EX LIBRIS

VINTAGE CLASSICS

Hurricanes in Perfect Power

EDITED BY

Candice Brathwaite

Hurricanes in Perfect Power

Tales of Modern Motherhood

EDITED BY
Candice Brathwaite

VINTAGE

1 3 5 7 9 10 8 6 4 2

Vintage Classics is part of the Penguin Random House
group of companies whose addresses can be found at
global.penguinrandomhouse.com

Introduction copyright © Candice Brathwaite, 2023

Project management by Anna Nightingale

This edition published in Vintage Classics in 2023

The acknowledgements page at the end of the book should
be seen as an extension of this copyright page

penguin.co.uk/vintage-classics

A CIP catalogue record for this book is available from the British Library

ISBN 9781784878313

Typeset in 13/18pt Adobe Jenson Pro by Jouve (UK), Milton Keynes
Printed and bound in Great Britain by Clays Ltd, Elcograf S.p.A.

The authorised representative in the EEA is Penguin Random House Ireland,
Morrison Chambers, 32 Nassau Street, Dublin D02 YH68

Penguin Random House is committed to a sustainable future
for our business, our readers and our planet. This book is made
from Forest Stewardship Council® certified paper.

MIX
Paper from
responsible sources
FSC® C018179

Contents

Introduction

Today as I begin to write this introduction it's as if Leto, the Greek goddess of motherhood herself, is heartily laughing at me, not with me.

The first of the school lurgies has entered our house. My husband is supporting our business elsewhere, meaning that I am currently balancing a laptop on my lap, a lukewarm cup of coffee in one hand and a bagel in the other, while always keeping one eye trained on a particularly energetic four-year-old whose temperature is sitting at 39°.

My eye, however trained it may be, slips out of focus if I look for long enough. Held within the blur is a moment in which the time I've spent as a mother to this child feels distant and present all at once. I think of those early days, when the heaviness of my tummy felt linked to my eyelids, my brain begging for sleep and my body praying for a miracle. My bones themselves felt exhausted. But this was my second child, so the repeated reassurance that 'they grow up so fast' was not a sound that resonated with the same impact. I had awoken to this truth once before. But oh, to wake up there again!

Through the years I've been serenaded by the soft moo of the breast pump or called upon abruptly by a sharp squeal the moment a toe touches bath water. I have a four-year-old, an almost-ten-year-old and a fourteen-year-old stepdaughter. I have had to acknowledge that modern motherhood is peppered with hurricanes, none of which feel as confronting as the first, but the smaller ones accumulate. They're all as life-altering as each other.

Over almost a decade I have faced the internal hurricane that comes with doing what's best for my children even if it comes at a personal sacrifice. In 'Winterscape' by Anita Desai, a biological mother lets her grieving, heartbroken sister nurture the child she'd given birth to out of love for them both. The story speaks of a bargain I couldn't imagine making, not just because I have strained relationships with similar characters in my own life, but because it's hard to imagine letting someone else raise your child when you've carried them and you too love and want them. Motherhood is filled with difficult decisions but, as Desai suggests, if they're driven by love more than ego, you will, more often than not, make the right one.

I have faced the agonising thought of not becoming a mother. Going through that has, I think, made me the mother I am now. While I doubt this was Ali Smith's intention in 'The Child', her story helped provide me with language for that period of my life. The piece also articulates an idea – and a fear – of motherhood, which stands in stark opposition to the ideals of those who want the best for their children: that nature may sometimes take precedent over nurture, and that your child, despite your very best efforts, might turn out to be the opposite of what you imagined. 'The Child' is a burlesque of this, whereby a baby is a cruel tyrant, expressing prejudiced views of women and asylum seekers.

And I have, of course, like the protagonist in Toni

Morrison's 'Sweetness', continued to tussle with the hurricane of being a black mother, with all its intricacies. Historically, black mothers haven't been given space in black British literature. I predict that this will be the longest lasting hurricane of all.

When I was asked to edit this book, I had no idea what kind of work I would read and how it would make me view my motherhood journey thus far. Having grown so tired of the microwave pop-and-go type motherhood books, I was more than willing to sink my teeth into words that would maybe, just maybe, help me more eloquently describe the indescribable.

What I love most about the stories I've chosen for this book is how far-reaching they are. It will always be important to me that stories and representations of motherhood are as diverse as possible. Even though my identity is one spread across many intersections, it doesn't cover all bases, and I too have had to learn what it means to be truly quiet and listen to someone else's version of motherhood – something we usually blanket as a universal experience. This is most true of 'Winning' by Casey Plett, about the relationship between a transgender mother and daughter.

Recently I was speaking to a friend who is a mother of two under two, who – let it be known – said she feels as though motherhood is either overly and falsely glamourised, or made out to be completely horrific, when actually there are multiple moments of each throughout the course of every single day. I couldn't help but agree.

While I don't regret my decision to embark on motherhood, I can firmly say that if I had been offered a one-year, no-holds-barred trial, I wouldn't currently be a mother of two.

The firm grip this duty has on my time, body and mental state, to say the least, is a stronghold that no one can actually describe. So many feel as though they cannot and should not communicate the pressures and stresses motherhood places on you, because it seems like every other mother is having a great time of it.

What's most striking about this collection of stories is how close they are to the blistering truth. They do not shy away. There aren't many saccharine moments – not because motherhood is without them, but because they are fleeting. Most of it is back-breaking emotional work, where the small beings you have made space for end up teaching you more than you bargained for.

In the days when my children were very young, I could have been a character in Helen Simpson's short story 'Café Society'. I remember all too well the tight-rope I walked daily between my life as a career woman, one where I felt independent for the hours between 9 and 5, and heading home to become a full-time carer to those who depended on me at night. I think back to when I preferred to walk four miles to meet a friend to avoid the countless buses that couldn't accommodate me. In fact, even if they could accommodate me, there were times that I would rather walk for miles with a pram than feel the prickles of a dozen corneas on me, all of them saying, without tongues, that they wished I could do a better job at keeping my baby quiet.

And then there are, of course, glimpses into future hurricanes. Unlike a meteorologist, I don't need apparatus to predict these ones. The hurricane of your children becoming emboldened enough to show you a reflection of yourself. The hurricanes that come alongside being their first bouncer, forcefully batting any harm out of the way as it comes hurtling towards the one thing you feel obliged to protect. This is explored in 'Mother's Son' by Tessa Hadley, where a son confides in his mother that he is having an affair with someone he loves, and the mother conceals this from her son's distressed girlfriend. The story articulates one of my bigger fears: becoming a woman who hurts other women by putting her instinctive, but arguably misplaced, loyalty to her son before all, even herself. As sure as I am in this moment that I would dissolve any twisted loyalty I think I have towards my son in order to protect someone else's daughter, I haven't yet been faced with this in real time. I hope that if I ever find myself there I can stand firm, but if there is one phrase that motherhood has taught me to live by, it's 'who knows?'.

It's after months of thinking about these stories and a week of writing that I'm drawing this introduction to a close. My time, like my body, is no longer my own; I'm bound by my children's schedules, which often become complicated by the unexpected, including my current battle with sickness. I do things incrementally, making things happen as and when I can.

I am now sitting in a clinical environment wearing a clean gown that perhaps hundreds if not thousands have worn before me. It feels symbolic of motherhood itself. After five years of suffering with terrible back passage issues after giving birth to a 10lb 2oz son, I've finally been forced to put myself first. I think that may be the thread that ties all of these beautiful, emotional, scary and sometimes heartbreaking stories together: a desire to remember oneself among becoming someone else's everything.

This collection stands as a reminder that there is not a single cell of newness that exists under the theme of motherhood. Someone has always been where we are or felt how we feel. In times of darkness, stories similar to ours can be hard to find, as traditional media and popular conversation parrots that motherhood is the greatest journey you will go on and that your child is the most precious gift. I hope you find that my selections for this book shine a light into all corners and resonate with mothers at every stage of their journey, from those of us with young children to those on the precipice of an empty nest; from those of us dealing with depression to those of us who can't wipe the smiles off of our faces. And I hope these stories hit home with those who aren't mothers, too. In some ways, I especially hope this collection reaches non-mothers. Because mothers and non-mothers have to co-exist in community spaces, those that we all depend on, and in this sense I hope this book can be used as an educational tool. I hope it offers entertainment as well as blistering insight into worlds that, for me as a mother, are commonplace but for so many are currently, and may forever remain, foreign. I hope that digesting these stories will help those who aren't familiar with the hurricane of motherhood understand just how much their support, help and understanding is desired, even needed, for all of us to feel good and be well.

Candice Brathwaite, 2023

Winterscape

by Anita Desai

She stands with the baby in her arms in front of the refrigerator, and points at the pictures she has taped on its white enamel surface, each in turn, calling out the names of the people in the photographs. It is a game they play often to pass the time, the great stretches of time they spend alone together. The baby jabs his short pink finger at a photograph, and the mother cries, 'That's Daddy, in his new car!' or 'Susan and cousin Ted, on his first birthday!' and 'Grandma by the Christmas tree!' All these pictures are as bright and festive as bits of tinsel or confetti. Everyone is smiling in them, and there are birthday cakes and Christmas trees, the shining chrome of new cars, bright green lawns and white houses. 'Da-dee!' the baby shouts. 'Soo-sun!' The bright colours make the baby smile. The mother is happy to play the game, and laughs: her baby is learning the names of all the members of the family; he is becoming a part of the family.

Then the baby reaches out and waves an ineffectual hand at a photograph that is almost entirely white, only a few shades of grey to bring out the shapes and figures in it. There are two, and both are draped in snow-white clothes which cover their shoulders, exposing only the backs of their heads which are white too, and they are standing beside the very same white refrigerator in the same white-painted kitchen, in front of a white-framed window. They are looking out of it, not at the camera but at the snow that is falling past the window-panes, covering the leafless tree and the wooden fence and the ground outside, providing them with a white snowscape into which they seem nearly to have merged. Nearly.

The baby's pink finger jabs at the white photograph. The mother says nothing immediately: she seems silenced, as if she too has joined the two figures at the window and with them is looking out of the white kitchen into a white world. The photograph somehow calls for silence, creates silence, like snow.

The baby too drops his hand, lowers his head on his mother's shoulder, and yawns. Snow, silence, and sleep: the white picture has filled him with sleep, he is overcome by it. His mother holds him and rocks him, swaying on her feet. She loves the feel of the baby's head on her shoulder; she tucks it under her chin protec-tively. She swivels around to the window as if she sees the two white figures there now, vanishing into the green dusk of a summer evening. She sings softly into the baby's dark hair: 'Ma and Masi – Ma and Masi together.'

'*Two?*' Beth turned her head on the pillow and stared at him over the top of her glasses, lowering the book she was reading to the rounded dome of her belly under the blue coverlet. '*Two* tickets? For *whom?*' because she knew Rakesh did not have a father, that his mother was a widow.

'For my mother and my aunt,' he said, in a low, almost sullen voice, sitting on the edge of the bed in his pyjamas and twisting his fingers together. His back was turned to her, his shoulders stooped. Because of the time difference, he had had to place the call to the village in India in the middle of the night.

'Your *aunt?*' Beth heard her own voice escalate. 'Why do we have to pay for your aunt to visit us? Why does *she* have to visit us when the baby is born? I can't have so many guests in the house, Rakesh!'

He turned around towards her slowly, and she saw dark circles under his eyes. Another time they might have caused her to put her finger out to touch those big, bluish pouches, like bruises, but now she felt herself tense at the thought of not just one, but two strangers, foreigners, part of Rakesh's past, invading their house. She had already wished she had not allowed Rakesh to send for his mother to attend to the birth of their child. It had seemed an outlandish, archaic idea even when it was first suggested; now it was positively bizarre. 'Why both of them? We only asked your mother,' she insisted.

Rakesh was normally quick with his smile, his reassuring words, soft and comforting murmurs. He had seemed nervous ever since she became pregnant, more inclined to worry about what she took as a natural process. But she could see it was not that, it was something else that made him brood, silently, on the edge of the bed, the blue pouches hanging under his eyes, and his hands twisted.

'What's the matter?' she said sharply, and took off her glasses and turned over her book. 'What's wrong?'

He roused himself to shake his head, attempted to smile, and failed. Then he lifted up his legs and lay down on the bed, beside her, turning to her with that same brooding expression, not really seeing her. He put out his hand and tried to stroke the hair at her temple. It annoyed her: he was so clearly about to make a request, a difficult request. She tensed, ready to refuse. He ought not to be asking anything of her in her condition. Two guests, two foreigners – at such a time. 'Tell me,' she demanded.

So he began to tell her. 'They are both my mothers, Beth,' he said. 'I have two mothers.'

*

4

There were three years between them and those seemed to have made all the difference. Asha was the first child in the family. So delighted was her father that it never crossed his mind she should have been a son. He tossed her up and caught her in his arms and put his face into her neck to make growling sounds that sent her into squeals of laughter. That she was fair-skinned, plump and had curly hair and bright black eyes all pleased him. He liked his wife to dress the child in frilly, flounced, flowered dresses and put ribbons in her hair. She was glad and relieved he was so pleased with his daughter: it could have been otherwise, but he said, 'A pretty daughter is an ornament to the home.'

So Asha grew up knowing she was an ornament, and a joy. She had no hesitation ever in asking for a toy or a sweet, in climbing onto her parents' laps or standing in the centre of a circle to sing or skip.

When Anu was born, three years later, it was different. Although her father bent over her and fondled her head and said nothing to express disappointment, disappointment was in the air. It swaddled baby Anu (no one even remembered her full name, the more majestic Annapurna), and among the first things she heard were the mutterings of the older people in the family who had no compunction about pronouncing their disappointment. And while her mother held her close and defended her against them, baby Anu knew she was in a weak position. So one might have thought, watching her grow. Although she stayed close to her elder sister, clinging to the hem of her dress, shadowing her, and Asha was pleased to have someone so entirely under her control, there remained something hesitant, nervous and tentative about Anu's steps, her movements and speech. Everything about her expressed diffidence.

While Asha proved a natural housekeeper and joined, with gusto, in the cooking, the washing, the sweeping, all those household tasks shared between the women, pinning her chunni back behind her ears, rolling up the sleeves of her kameez, and settling down to kneading the dough, or pounding spices, or rolling out chapatis with a fine vigour, Anu proved sadly incompetent. She managed to get her hand burnt when frying pakoras, took so long to grind chillies that her mother grew impatient and pushed her out of the way, and was too weak to haul up a full bucket of water from the well, needing to do it half a bucket at a time. When visitors filled the house and everything was in an uproar, Anu would try to slip away and make herself invisible and only return when summoned – to be scolded soundly for shirking work. 'Look at your sister,' she was always counselled, and she did, raising her eyes with timid admiration. Asha, used to her sister's ways, gave her a wink and slipped her one of the snacks or sweets she had missed. An understanding grew between them, strengthened by strand upon strand upon strand of complicity.

Later, sons were born to their parents, and the pressure, the tension in their relationships with their daughters was relieved. Good-naturedly, the father allowed both of them to go to school. 'What is the harm?' he asked the elderly critics of this unusual move. 'These days it is good for girls to be educated. One day, who knows, they may work in an office – or a bank!'

That certainly did not happen. Another generation would be born and raised before any girl in that Punjab village became an office clerk or a bank teller. Asha and Anu had a few years in the local government school where they wore blue cotton kameezes with white chunnis, and white gym shoes, and sat on benches learning the Punjabi alphabet and their numbers. Here the scales may well have tipped the other way, because Asha found the work ferociously difficult and grew hot and bothered as she tried to work out problems in addition and subtraction or to read her lessons from the tattered, illustrated textbooks, while Anu discovered an unexpected nimbleness of mind that skipped about the numbers with the agility of a young goat, and scampered through the letters quite friskily. Asha threw her sister exasperated looks but did not mind so much when Anu took over her homework and did it for her in her beautiful hand. Anu drew praise when she wrote essays on 'The Cow' and 'My Favourite Festival' – but, alas, the latter proved to be her swan song because at this point Asha turned fifteen and the family found her a bridegroom and married her off and Anu had to stay home from then on to help her mother.

Asha's bridegroom was a large man, not so young, but it did not matter because he owned so much land and cattle. He had a great handlebar moustache and a turban and Anu was terrified for Asha when she first saw him, but was later to find no cause for terror: he was a kindly, good-natured man who clearly adored his bright-eyed, quick-tongued, lively young wife and was generous to her and to her entire family. His voice was unexpectedly soft and melodious, and he often regaled his visitors, or a gathering in the village, with his songs. Asha – who had plenty of talents but not artistic ones – looked at him with admiration then, sitting back on her haunches and cupping her chin in her hands which were bedecked with the rings and brace-lets he had given her.

They often asked Anu to come and stay with them. Asha found she was so accustomed to having her younger sister at her heels, she really could not do with-out her. She might have done, had she had children, but, though many were born to her, they were either stillborn or died soon after birth, none living for more than a few days. This created an emptiness in the big house so full of goods and comforts, and Asha grew querulous and plaintive, a kind of bitterness informing her every gesture and expression, while her husband became prone to depression which no one would have predicted earlier. Anu often came upon him seated in an armchair at the end of the veranda, or up on the flat roof of the house in the cool evenings, looking out with an expression of deep melancholy across his fields to the horizon where the white spire and the golden dome of the Sikh temple stood against the sky. He left the work on the farm to a trusted head-man to supervise and became idle himself, exasperating Asha who tended to throw herself into every possible activity with determined vigour and thought a man should too.

After yet another miscarriage, Asha roused herself with a grim wilfulness to join in the preparation for Anu's wedding, arranged by the parents to a clerk in a neighbouring town, a sullen, silent young man with large teeth and large hands that he rubbed together all the time. Anu kept her face and her tears hidden throughout the wedding, as brides did, and Asha was both consoling and encouraging, as women were.

Unexpectedly, that unpromising young man, who blinked through his spectacles and could scarcely croak one sentence at a time, showed no hesitation whatsoever when it came to fathering a child. Nor did Anu,

9

who was so slight of frame and mousy in manner, seem to be in any way handicapped as a woman or mother – her child was born easily, and it was a son. A round, black-haired, red-cheeked boy who roared lustily for his milk and thrashed out with his legs and grabbed with his hands, clearly meant for survival and success.

If Anu and her husband were astonished by him, it could scarcely have matched Asha and her husband's wonder. They were enthralled by the boy: he was the child of their dreams, their thwarted hopes and desires. Anu lay back and watched how Asha scooped Rakesh up into her large, soft arms, how she cradled and kissed him, then how her husband took him from her, wrapped in the candy pink wool shawl knitted by Asha, and crooned over him. She was touched and grateful for Asha's competence, as adept at handling the baby as in churning butter or making sweets. Anu stayed in bed, letting her sister fuss over both her and the baby – making Anu special milk and almond and jaggery drinks in tall metal tumblers, keeping the baby happy and content, massaging him with mustard oil, feeding him sips of sweetened milk from a silver shell, tickling him till he smiled.

Anu's husband looked on, awkwardly, too nervous to hold his own child: small creatures made him afraid; he never failed to kick a puppy or a kitten out of his way, fiercely. Anu rose from her bed occasionally to make a few tentative gestures of motherhood but soon relinquished them, one by one, first letting Asha feed the baby and dress him, then giving up attempts to nurse the boy and letting Asha take over the feeding.

At the first hint of illness – actually, the baby was teething which caused a tummy upset – Asha bundled him up in his blanket and took him home, promising, 'I'll bring him back as soon as he is well. Now you go and rest, Anu, you haven't slept and you look sick yourself.'

When Anu went to fetch him after a week, she came upon Asha's husband, sitting on that upright chair of his on the veranda, but now transformed. He had the baby on his knee and was hopping him up and down while singing a rhyme, and his eyes sparkled as vivaciously as the child's. Instead of taking her son from him, Anu held back, enjoying the scene. Noticing her at last, the large man in the turban beamed at her. 'A prince!' he said. 'And one day he will have all my fields, my cattle, the dairy, the cane-crushing factory, everything. He will grow up to be a prince!'

Rakesh's first birthday was to be celebrated at Asha's house – 'We will do it in style,' she said, revealing how little she thought Anu and her husband were capable of achieving it. Preparations went on for weeks beforehand. There was to be a feast for the whole village. A goat was to be slaughtered and roasted, and the women in the family were busy making sweets and delicacies with no expense spared: Asha's husband was seeing to that. He himself went out to shoot partridges for the festive dinner, setting out before dawn into the rippling grainfields and calling back to the women to have the fire ready for his return.

Those were his last words – to have the fire ready. 'As if he knew', wept Asha's mother, 'that it was the funeral pyre we would light.' Apparently there had been an accident with the gun. It had gone off unexpectedly and the bullet had pierced his shoulder and a lung: he had bled to death. There were no birthday festivities for one-year-old Rakesh.

Knowing that the one thing that could comfort Asha was the presence of the baby in her arms, Anu refrained from suggesting she take him home. At first, she had planned to leave the boy with her widowed sister for the first month of mourning, then drew it out to two and even three months. When her husband, taunted by his own family for his failure to establish himself as head of his household, ordered her to bring their son home, Anu surprised herself by answering, 'Let him be. Asha needs him. We can have more sons for ourselves.' Their house was empty and melancholy – it had always been a mean place, a narrow set of rooms in the bazaar, with no sunlight or air – but she sat in its gloom, stitching clothes for her rapidly growing son, a chunni drawn over her head, a picture of acceptance that her husband was not able to disturb, except briefly, with fits of violence.

After one of these, they would go and visit the boy, with gifts, and Rakesh came to look upon his parents as a visiting aunt and uncle, who offered him sweets and toys with a dumbly appeasing, appealing air. No one remembered when he started calling them Masi and Masa. Asha he already addressed as Ma: it was so clearly her role.

Anu had been confident other children would follow. She hoped for a daughter next time, somehow feeling a daughter might be more like her, and more likely to stay with her. But Rakesh had his second and third birthday in Asha's house, and there was no other child. Anu's husband looked discouraged now, and resentful, his own family turning into a chorus of mocking voices. He stayed away at work for long hours; there were rumours – quickly brought to Anu's attention – that he had taken to gambling, and drugs, and some even hinted at having seen him in quarters of the town where respectable people did not go. She was not too perturbed: their relationship was a furtive, nocturnal thing that never survived daylight. She was concerned, of course, when he began to look ill, to break out in boils and rashes, and come down with frequent fevers, and she nursed him in her usual bungling, tentative way. His family came to take over, criticizing her sharply for her failings as a nurse, but he only seemed to grow worse, and died shortly before Rakesh's fifth birthday. His family set up a loud lament and clearly blamed her for the way he had dwindled away in spite of their care. She packed her belongings – in the same tin trunk in which she had brought them as a bride, having added nothing more to them – and went to live with Asha – and the child.

In the dark, Beth found it was she who was stroking the hair at Rakesh's temple now, and he who lay stretched out with his hands folded on his chest and his eyes staring at the ceiling.

'Then the woman you call Ma – she is really your aunt?' Beth queried.

Rakesh gave a long sigh. 'I always knew her as my mother.'

'And your aunt is your real mother? When did they tell you?'

'I don't know,' he admitted. 'I grew up knowing it – perhaps people spoke of it in the village, but when you are small you don't question. You just accept.'

'But didn't your *real* mother ever tell you, or try to take you away?'

'No!' he exclaimed. 'That's just it, Beth. She never did – she had given me to her sister, out of love, out of

14

sympathy when her husband died. She never tried to break up the relationship I had with her. It was out of love.' He tried to explain again, 'The love sisters feel.'

Beth, unlike Rakesh, had a sister. Susan. She thought of her now, living with her jobless, worthless husband in a trailer somewhere in Manitoba with a string of children. The thought of handing over her child to her was so bizarre that it made her snort. 'I know I couldn't give my baby to Susan for anything,' she declared, removing her hand from his temple and placing it on her belly.

'You don't know, you can't say – what may happen, what things one may do—'

'*Of course* I know,' she said, more loudly. 'Nothing, no one, could make me do that. Give my baby away?' Her voice became shrill and he turned on his side, closing his eyes to show her he did not wish to continue the conversation.

She understood that gesture but she persisted. 'But didn't they ever fight? Or disagree about the way you were brought up? Didn't they have different ideas of how to do that? You know, I've told Susan—'

He sighed again. 'It was not like that. They understood each other. Ma looked after me – she cooked for me and fed me, made me sit down on a mat and sat in front of me and fed me with her own hands. And what a cook she is! Beth, you'll love—' he broke off, knowing he was going too far, growing foolish now. 'And Masi,' he recovered himself, 'she took me by the hand to school. In the evening, she lit the lamp and made me show her my books. She helped me with my lessons – and I think learned with me. She is a reader, Beth, like you,' he was able to say with greater confidence.

'But weren't they jealous of each other – of one for cooking for you and feeding you, and the other for sharing your lessons? Each was doing what the other didn't, after all.'

He caught her hand, on the coverlet, to stop her talking. 'It wasn't like that,' he said again, and wished she would be silent so he could remember for himself that brick-walled courtyard in the village, the pump gushing out the sweet water from the tube well, the sounds of cattle stirring in the sheaves of fodder in the sheds, the can of frothing milk the dairyman brought to the door, the low earthen stove over which his mother – his aunt – stirred a pan in the smoky dimness of dawn, making him tea. The pigeons in the rafters, cooing, a feather drifting down –

'Well, I suppose I'll be seeing them both, then – and I'll find out for myself,' Beth said, a bit grimly, and snapped off the light.

'Never heard of anything so daft,' pronounced her mother, pouring out a cup of coffee for Beth who sat at her kitchen table with her elbows on its plastic cover and her chin cupped in her hands. Doris was still in her housecoat and slippers, going about her morning in the sunlit kitchen. Beth had come early.

When Beth did not reply, Doris planted her hands on the table and stared into her brooding face. 'Well, isn't it?' she demanded. 'Whoever heard of such a thing? Rakesh having two mothers! Why ever didn't he tell us before?'

'He told me about them both of course,' Beth flared up, and began to stir her coffee. 'He talked of them as his mother and aunt. I knew they were both widows, lived together, that's all.'

Doris looked as if she had plenty more to say on the subject than that. She tightened the belt around her red-striped house-coat and sat down squarely across from Beth. 'Looks as if he never told you who his mother was though, or his father. The real ones, I mean. I call that peculiar, Beth, pec-u-liar!'

Beth stirred resentfully. 'I s'pose he hardly thinks of it that way – he was a baby when it happened. He says he grew up just accepting it. They *love* each other, he said.'

Doris scratched at her head with one hand, rattled the coffee cup in its saucer with the other. 'Two sisters loving each other – that much? That's what's so daft – who in her right mind would give away her baby to her sister just like that? I mean, would you hand yours over to Susan? And would Susan take it? I mean, as if it were a birthday present!'

'Oh, Mum!'

'Now you've spilt your coffee! Wait, I'll get a sponge. Don't get up. You're getting big, girl. You OK? You mustn't mind me.'

'I'm OK, Mum, but now I'm going to have two women visiting. Rakesh's mum would be one thing, but two of 'em together – I don't know.'

'That's what I say,' Doris added quickly. 'And all that expense – why's he sending them tickets? I thought they had money: he keeps talking about that farm as if they were landlords—'

'Oh, that's where he grew up, Mum. They sold it long ago – that's what paid for his education at McGill, you know. That costs.'

'What – it cost them the whole farm? He's always talking about how big it was—'

'They sold it a bit at a time. They helped pay for our house, too, and then set up his practice.'

'Hmm,' said Doris, as she shook a cigarette out of a packet and put it in her mouth.

'Oh, Mum, I can't stand smoke now! It makes me nauseous – you know that—' Beth protested.

'Sorry, love,' Doris said, and laid down the match-box she had picked up but with the cigarette still between her lips. 'I'm just worried about you – dealing with two Indian women – in your condition—'

'I guess they know about babies,' Beth said hopefully.

'But do they know about Canada?' Doris came back smartly, as one who had learnt. 'And about the Canadian *winter*?'

They thought they did – from Rakesh's dutiful, although not very informative, letters over the years. After Rakesh had graduated from the local college, it was Asha who insisted he go abroad 'for further studies'. Anu would not have had the courage to suggest it, and had no money of her own to spend, but here was another instance of her sister's courage and boldness. Asha had seen all the bright young people of the village leave and told Anu, 'He' – meaning her late husband – 'wanted Rakesh to study abroad. "We will give him the best education," he had said, so I am only doing what he told me to.' She tucked her widow's white chunni behind her ears and lifted her chin, looking proud. When Anu raised the matter of expense, she waved her hand – so competent at raising the boy, at running the farm, and now at handling the accounts. 'We will sell some of the land. Where is the need for so much? Rakesh will never be a farmer,' she said. So Rakesh began to apply to foreign universities, and although his two mothers felt tightness in their chests at the prospect of his leaving them, they also swelled with pride to think he might do so, the first in the family to leave the country 'for further studies'. When he had completed his studies – the two women selling off bits and pieces of the land to pay for them till there was nothing left but the old farmhouse – he wrote to tell them he had been offered jobs by several firms. They wiped their eyes with the corners of their chunnis, weeping for joy at his success and the sorrowful knowledge that he would not come back. Instead, they received letters about his achievements: his salary, his promotion, and with it the apartment in the city, then his own office and practice, photographs accompanying each as proof.

Then, one day, the photograph that left them speechless: it showed him standing with his arm around a girl, a blonde girl, at an office party. She was smiling. She had fair hair cut short and wore a green hairband and a green dress. Rakesh was beaming. He had grown rather fat, his stomach bulging out of a striped shirt, above a leather belt with a big buckle. He was also rather bald. The girl looked small and slim and young beside him. Rakesh did not tell them how old she was, what family she came from, what schooling she had had, when was the wedding, should they come, and other such particulars of importance to them.

Rakesh, when he wrote, managed to avoid almost all such particulars, mentioning only that the wedding would be small, merely an official matter of registration at the town hall, they need not trouble to come – as they had ventured to suggest.

They were hurt. They tried to hide it from their neighbours as they went around with boxes of tinsel-spread sweets as gifts to celebrate the far-off occasion. So when the letter arrived announcing Beth's punctual pregnancy and the impending birth, they did not again make the mistake of tactful enquiries: Anu's letter stated with unaccustomed boldness their intention to travel to Canada and see their grandchild for themselves. That was her term – 'our grandchild'.

Yet it was with the greatest trepidation that they set out on this adventure. Everyone in the village was encouraging and supportive. Many of them had flown to the US, to Canada, to England, to visit their children abroad. It had become almost commonplace for the families to travel to New Delhi, catch a plane and fly off to some distant continent, bearing bundles and boxes full of the favourite pickles, chutneys and sweets of their far-flung progeny. Stories abounded of these goodies being confiscated on arrival at the airports, taken away by indignant customs officers to be burnt: 'He asked me, "What is *this*? What is *this*?" He had never seen mango pickle before, can you believe?' 'He didn't know what is betel nut! "Beetle? You are bringing in an insect?" he asked!' – and of being stranded at airports by great blizzards or lightning strikes by airline staff – 'We were lucky we had taken our bedroll and could spread out on the floor and sleep' – and of course they vied with each other with reports of their sons' and daughters' palatial mansions, immense cars, stocked refrigerators, prodigies of shopping in the most extensive of department stores. They brought back with them electrical appliances, cosmetics, watches, these symbols of what was 'foreign'.

The two mothers had taken no part in this, saying, 'We can get those here too,' and contenting themselves by passing around the latest photographs of Rakesh and his wife and their home in Toronto. Now that they too were to join this great adventure, they became nervous – even Asha did. Young, travelled daughters and granddaughters of old friends came around to reassure them: 'Auntie, it is not difficult at all! Just buy a ticket at the booth, put it in the slot, and step into the subway. It will take you where you like,' or 'Over there you won't need kerosene or coal for the stove, Auntie. You have only to switch on the stove, it will light by itself,' or 'You won't need to wash your clothes, Auntie. They have machines, you put everything in, with soap, it washes by itself.' The two women wondered if these self-confident youngsters were pulling their legs: they were not reassured. Every piece of information, meant to help, threw them into greater agitation. They were convinced they would be swallowed up by the subway if they went out, or electrocuted at home if they stayed in. By the time the day of their departure came around, they were feverish with anxiety and sleeplessness. Anu would gladly have abandoned the plan – but Asha reminded her that Rakesh had sent them tickets, his first present to them after leaving home, how could they refuse?

It was ten years since Rakesh had seen his mothers, and he had forgotten how thinly they tended to dress, how unequipped they might be. Beth's first impression of them as they came out of the immigration control area, wheeling a trolley between them with their luggage precariously balanced on it, was of their wisps of widows' white clothing – muslin, clearly – and slippers flapping at their feet. Rakesh was embarrassed by their skimpy apparel, Beth unexpectedly moved. She had always thought of them as having so much; now her reaction was: they have so little!

She took them to the stores at once to fit them out with overcoats, gloves, mufflers – and woollen socks. They drew the line at shoes: they had never worn shoes, could not fit their feet into them, insisting on wearing their sandals with thick socks instead. She brought them back barely able to totter out of the car and up the drive, weighed down as they were by great duffel coats that kept their arms lifted from their sides, with their hands fitted into huge gloves, and with their heads almost invisible under the wrappings of woollen mufflers. Under it all, their white cotton kameezes hung out like rags of their past, sadly.

When Doris came around to visit them, she brought along all the spare blankets she had in her apartment, presciently. 'Thought you'd be cold,' she told them. 'I went through the war in England, and I know what that's like, I can tell you. And it isn't half cold yet. Wait till it starts to snow.' They smiled eagerly, in polite anticipation.

While Beth and Doris bustled about, 'settling them in', Rakesh stood around, unexpectedly awkward and ill at ease. After the first ecstatic embrace and the deep breath of their lingering odour of the barnyard and woodsmoke and the old soft muslin of their clothing, their sparse hair, he felt himself in their way and didn't know quite what to do with himself or with them. It was Beth who made them tea and tested their English while Rakesh sat with his feet apart, cracking his knuckles and smiling somewhat vacantly.

At the table, it was different: his mothers unpacked all the foods they had brought along, tied up in small bundles or packed in small boxes, and coaxed him to eat, laughing as they remembered how he had pestered them for these as a child. To them, he was still that: a child, and now he ate, and a glistening look of remembrance covered his face like a film of oil on his fingers, but he also glanced sideways at Beth, guiltily, afraid of betraying any disloyalty to her. She wrinkled her nose slightly, put her hand on her belly and excused herself from eating on account of her pregnancy. They nodded sympathetically and promised to make special preparations for her.

On weekends, Beth insisted he take them out and show them the sights, and they dutifully allowed themselves to be led into his car, and then around museums, up radio towers and into department stores – but they tended to become carsick on these excursions, foot-weary in museums and confused in stores. They clearly preferred to stay in. That was painful, and the only way out of the boredom was to bring home videos and put them on. Then everyone could put their heads back and sleep, or pretend to sleep.

On weekdays, in desperation, Beth too took to switching on the television set, tuned to programmes she surmised were blandly innocent, and imagined they would sit together on the sofa and find amusement in the nature, travel and cooking programmes. Unfortunately, these had a way of changing when her back was turned and she would return to find them in a state of shock from watching a torrid sex scene or violent battle taking place before their affronted and disbelieving eyes. They sat side by side with their feet dangling and their eyes screwed up, munching on their dentures with fear at the popping of guns, the exploding of bombs and grunting of naked bodies. Their relief when she suggested a break for tea was palpable. Once in the kitchen, the kettle whistling shrilly, cups standing ready with the threads of tea bags dangling out of them, they seemed reluctant to leave the sanctuary. The kitchen was their great joy, once they had got used to the shiny enamel and chrome and up-to-date gadgetry. They became expert at punching the buttons of the microwave although they never learnt what items could and what could not be placed in it. To Rakesh's surprise it was Anu who seemed to comprehend the rules better, she who peered at any scrap of writing, trying to decipher some meaning. Together the two would open the refrigerator twenty times in one morning, never able to resist looking in at its crowded, illuminated shelves; that reassurance of food seemed to satisfy them on some deep level – their eyes gleamed and they closed the door on it gently, with a dreamy expression.

Still, the resources of the kitchen were not limitless. Beth found they had soon run through them, and the hours dragged for her, in the company of the two mothers. There were just so many times she could ask Doris to come over and relieve her, and just so many times she could invent errands that would allow them all to escape from the house so crowded with their hopes, expectations, confusion and disappointments. She knew Rakesh disappointed them. She watched them trying to recreate what he had always described to her as his most warmly close and intimate relationship, and invariably failing. The only way they knew to do this was to cook him the foods of his childhood – as best they could reproduce these in this strange land – or retail the gossip of the village, not realising he had forgotten the people they spoke of, had not the slightest interest in who had married whom, or sold land or bought cattle. He would give embarrassed laughs, glance at Beth in appeal, and find reasons to stay late at work. She was exasperated by his failure but also secretly relieved to see how completely he had transformed himself into a husband, a Canadian, and, guiltily, she too dragged out her increasingly frequent escapes – spending the afternoon at her mother's house, describing to a fascinated Doris the village ways of these foreign mothers, or meeting girlfriends for coffee, going to the library to read child-rearing manuals – then returning in a rush of concern for the two imprisoned women at home.

*

She had spent one afternoon at the library, deep in an old stuffed chair in an undisturbed corner she knew, reading – something she found she could not do at home where the two mothers would watch her as she read, intently, as if waiting to see where it would take her and when she would be done – when she became aware of the light fading, darkness filling the tall window under which she sat. When she looked up, she was startled to see flakes of snow drifting through the dark, minute as tiny bees flying in excited hordes. They flew faster and faster as she watched, and in no time they would grow larger, she knew. She closed the magazine hastily, replaced it on the rack, put on her beret and gloves, picked up her bag and went out to the car. She opened the door and got in clumsily; she was so large now it was difficult to fit behind the steering wheel.

The streets were very full, everyone hurrying home before the snowfall became heavier. Her windscreen wiper going furiously, Beth drove home carefully. The first snowfall generally had its element of surprise; something childish in her responded with excitement. But this time she could only think of how surprised the two mothers would be, how much more intense their confinement.

When she let herself into the house with her key, she could look straight down the hall to the kitchen, and there she saw them standing, at the window, looking out to see the snow collect on the twigs and branches of the bare cherry tree and the tiles of the garden shed and the top of the wooden fence outside. Their white cotton saris were wrapped about them like shawls, their two heads leant against each other as they peered out, speechlessly.

They did not hear her, they were so absorbed in the falling of the snow and the whitening of the stark scene on the other side of the glass pane. She shut the door silently, slipped into her bedroom and fetched the camera from where it lay on the closet shelf. Then she came out into the hall again and, standing there, took a photograph.

Later, when it was developed – together with the first pictures of the baby – she showed the mothers the print, and they put their hands to their mouths in astonishment. 'Why didn't you tell us?' they said. 'We didn't know – our backs were turned.' Beth wanted to tell them it didn't matter, it was their postures that expressed everything, but then they would have wanted to know what 'everything' was, and she found she did not want to explain, she did not want words to break the silent completeness of that small, still scene. It was as complete, and as fragile, after all, as a snow crystal.

The birth of the baby broke through it, of course. The sisters revived as if he were a reincarnation of Rakesh.

They wanted to hold him, flat on the palms of their hands, or sit crosslegged on the sofa and rock him by pumping one knee up and down, and could not at all understand why Beth insisted they place him in his cot in a darkened bedroom instead. 'He has to learn to go to sleep by himself,' she told them when he cried and cried in protest and she refused to give them permission to snatch him up to their flat bosoms and console him.

They could not understand the rituals of baby care that Beth imposed – the regular feeding and sleeping times, the boiling and sterilizing of bottles and teats, the cans of formula and the use of disposable diapers. The first euphoria and excitement soon led to little nervous dissensions and explosions, then to dejection. Beth was too absorbed in her child to care.

The winter proved too hard, too long for the visitors. They began to fall ill, to grow listless, to show signs of depression and restlessness. Rakesh either did not notice or pretended not to, so that when Beth spoke of it one night in their bedroom, he asked if she were not 'overreacting', one of his favourite terms. 'Ask them, just ask them,' she retorted. 'How can I?' he replied. 'Can I say to them "D'you want to go home?" They'll think I want them to.' She flung her arms over her head in exasperation. 'Why can't you just talk to each other?' she asked.

She was restless too, eager to bring to an end a visit that had gone on too long. The two little old women were in her way, underfoot, as she hurried between cot and kitchen. She tried to throw them sympathetic smiles but knew they were more like grimaces. She often thought about the inexplicable relationship of these two women, how Masi, small, mousy Masi, had borne Rakesh and then given him over to Ma, her sister. What could have made her do that? How could she have? Thinking of her own baby, the way he filled her arms and fitted against her breast, Beth could not help but direct a piercing, perplexed stare at them. She knew she would not give up her baby for anything, anyone, certainly not to her sister Susan who was hardly capable of bringing up her own, and yet these two had lived their lives ruled by that one impulse, totally unnatural to her. They looked back at her, questioningly, sensing her hostility.

And eventually they asked Rakesh – very hesitantly, delicately, but clearly after having discussed the matter between themselves and having come to a joint decision. They wanted to go home. The baby had arrived safely, and Beth was on her feet again, very much so. And it was too much for her, they said, a strain. No, no, she had not said a thing, of course not, nothing like that, and nor had he, even inadvertently. They were happy – they had been happy – but now – and they coughed and coughed, in embarrassment as much as on account of the cold. And out of pity he cut short their fumbling explanations, and agreed to book their seats on a flight home. Yes, he and Beth would come and visit them, with the baby, as soon as he was old enough to travel.

This was the right thing to say. Their creased faces lifted up to him in gratitude. He might have spilt some water on wilting plants: they revived; they smiled; they began to shop for presents for everyone at home. They began to think of those at home, laugh in anticipation of seeing home again.

At the farewell in the airport – he took them there while Beth stayed at home with the baby, who had a cold – they cast their tender, grateful looks upon him again, then turned to wheel their trolley with its boxes and trunks away, full of gifts for family and neighbours. He watched as their shoulders, swathed in their white chunnis, and their bent white heads, turned away from him and disappeared. He lifted a fist to his eyes in an automatic gesture, then sighed with relief and headed for his car waiting in the grey snow.

At home, Beth had put the baby to sleep in his cot. She had cooked dinner, and on hearing Rakesh enter, she lit candles on the table, as though it were a celebration. He looked at her questioningly but she only smiled. She had cooked his favourite pasta. He sat at the table and lifted his fork, trying to eat. Why, what was she celebrating? He found a small, annoying knot of resentment fastened onto the fork at her evident pleasure at being alone with him and her baby again. He kept the fork suspended to look at her, to demand if this were so, and then saw, over her shoulder, the refrigerator with its array of the photographs and memos she liked to tape to its white enamel surface. What caught his eye was the photograph she had newly taped to it – with the view of the white window, and the two widows in white, and the whirling snow.

He put down his forkful of pasta. 'Rakesh? Rakesh?' Beth asked a few times, then turned to look herself. Together they stared at the winterscape.

'Why?' he asked.

Beth shrugged. 'Let it be,' she said.

What You Learn About the Baby

by Lydia Davis

Idle

You learn how to be idle, how to do nothing. That is the new thing in your life—to do nothing. To do nothing and not be impatient about doing nothing. It is easy to do nothing and become impatient. It is not easy to do nothing and not mind it, not mind the hours passing, the hours of the morning passing and then the hours of the afternoon, and one day passing and the next passing, while you do nothing.

What You Can Count On

You learn never to count on anything being the same from day to day, that he will fall asleep at a certain hour, or sleep for a certain length of time. Some days he sleeps for several hours at a stretch, other days he sleeps no more than half an hour.

Sometimes he will wake suddenly, crying hard, when you were prepared to go on working for another hour. Now you prepare to stop. But as it takes you a few minutes to end your work for the day, and you cannot go to him immediately, he stops crying and continues quiet. Now, though you have prepared to end work for the day, you prepare to resume working.

Don't Expect to Finish Anything

You learn never to expect to finish anything. For example, the baby is staring at a red ball. You are cleaning some large radishes. The baby will begin to fuss when you have cleaned four and there are eight left to clean.

You Will Not Know What Is Wrong

The baby is on his back in his cradle crying. His legs are slightly lifted from the surface of his mattress in the effort of his crying. His head is so heavy and his legs so light and his muscles so hard that his legs fly up easily from the mattress when he tenses, as now.

Often, you will wonder what is wrong, why he is crying, and it would help, it would save you much disturbance, to know what is wrong, whether he is hungry, or tired, or bored, or cold, or hot, or uncomfortable in his clothes, or in pain in his stomach or bowels. But you will not know, or not when it would help to know, at the time, but only later, when you have guessed correctly or many times incorrectly.

And it will not help to know afterwards, or it will not help unless you have learned from the experience to identify a particular cry that means hunger, or pain, etc. But the memory of a cry is a difficult one to fix in your mind.

What Exhausts You

You must think and feel for him as well as for yourself— that he is tired, or bored, or uncomfortable.

Sitting Still

You learn to sit still. You learn to stare as he stares, to stare up at the rafters as long as he stares up at the rafters, sitting still in a large space.

Entertainment

For him, though not usually for you, merely to look at a thing is an entertainment.

Then, there are some things that not just you, and not just he, but both of you like to do, such as lie in the hammock, or take a walk, or take a bath.

Renunciation

You give up, or postpone, for his sake, many of the pleasures you once enjoyed, such as eating meals when you are hungry, eating as much as you want, watching a movie all the way through from beginning to end, reading as much of a book as you want to at one sitting, going to sleep when you are tired, sleeping until you have had enough sleep.

You look forward to a party as you never used to look forward to a party, now that you are at home alone with him so much. But at this party you will not be able to talk to anyone for more than a few minutes, because he cries so constantly, and in the end he will be your only company, in a back bedroom.

Questions

How do his eyes know to seek out your eyes? How does his mouth know it is a mouth, when it imitates yours?

His Perceptions

You learn from reading it in a book that he recognizes you not by the appearance of your face but by your smell and the way you hold him, that he focuses clearly on an object only when it is held a certain distance from him, and that he can see only in shades of gray. Even what is white or black to you is only a shade of gray to him.

The Difficulty of a Shadow

He reaches to grasp the shadow of his spoon, but the shadow reappears on the back of his hand.

His Sounds

You discover that he makes many sounds in his throat to accompany what is happening to him: sounds in the form of grunts, air expelled in small gusts. Then sometimes high squeaks, and then sometimes, when he has learned to smile at you, high coos.

Priority

It should be very simple: while he is awake, you care for him. As soon as he goes to sleep, you do the most important thing you have to do, and do it as long as you can, either until it is done or until he wakes up. If he wakes up before it is done, you care for him until he sleeps again, and then you continue to work on the most important thing. In this way, you should learn to recognize which thing is the most important and to work on it as soon as you have the opportunity.

Odd Things You Notice About Him

The dark gray lint that collects in the lines of his palm.

The white fuzz that collects in his armpit.

The black under the tips of his fingernails. You have let his nails get too long, because it is hard to make a precise cut on such a small thing constantly moving. Now it would take a very small nailbrush to clean them.

The colors of his face: his pink forehead, his bluish

eyelids, his reddish-gold eyebrows. And the tiny beads of sweat standing out from the tiny pores of his skin.

When he yawns, how the wings of his nostrils turn yellow.

When he holds his breath and pushes down on his diaphragm, how quickly his face turns red.

His uneven breath: how his breath changes in response to his motion, and to his curiosity.

How his bent arms and legs, when he is asleep on his stomach, take the shape of an hourglass.

When he lies against your chest, how he lifts his head to look around like a turtle and drops it again because it is so heavy.

How his hands move slowly through the air like crabs or other sea creatures before closing on a toy.

How, bottom up, folded, he looks as though he were going away, or as though he were upside down.

Connected by a Single Nipple

You are lying on the bed nursing him, but you are not holding on to him with your arms or hands and he is not holding on to you. He is connected to you by a single nipple.

Disorder

You learn that there is less order in your life now. Or if there is to be order, you must work hard at maintaining it. For instance, it is evening and you are lying on the bed with the baby half asleep beside you. You are watching *Gaslight*. Suddenly a thunderstorm breaks and the rain comes down hard. You remember the baby's clothes out on the line, and you get up from the bed and run outdoors. The baby begins crying at being left so abruptly half asleep on the bed. *Gaslight* continues, the baby screams now, and you are out in the hard rainfall in your white bathrobe.

Protocol

There are so many occasions for greetings in the course of his day. Upon each waking, a greeting. Each time you enter the room, a greeting. And in each greeting there is real enthusiasm.

Distraction

You decide you must attend some public event, say a concert, despite the difficulty of arranging such a thing. You make elaborate preparations to leave the baby with a babysitter, taking a bag full of equipment, a folding bed, a folding stroller, and so on. Now, as the concert proceeds, you sit thinking not about the concert but only about the elaborate preparations and whether they have been adequate, and no matter how often you try to listen to the concert, you will hear only a few minutes of it before thinking again about those elaborate preparations and whether they have been adequate to the comfort of the baby and the convenience of the babysitter.

Henri Bergson

He demonstrates to you what you learned long ago from reading Henri Bergson—that laughter is always preceded by surprise.

You Do Not Know When He Will Fall Asleep

If his eyes are wide open staring at a light, it does not mean that he will not be asleep within minutes.

If he cries with a squeaky cry and squirms with wiry strength against your chest, digging his sharp little fingernails into your shoulder, or raking your neck, or pushing his face into your shirt, it does not mean he will not relax in five minutes and grow heavy. But five minutes is a very long time when you are caring for a baby.

What Resembles His Cry

Listening for his cry, you mistake, for his cry, the wind, seagulls, and police sirens.

Time

It is not that five minutes is always a very long time when you are caring for a baby but that time passes very slowly when you are waiting for a baby to go to sleep, when you are listening to him cry alone in his bed or whimper close to your ear.

Then time passes very quickly once the baby is asleep. The things you have to do have always taken this long to do, but before the baby was born it did not matter, because there were many such hours in the day to do these things. Now there is only one hour, and again later, on some days, one hour, and again, very late in the day, on some days, one last hour.

Order

You cannot think clearly or remain calm in such disorder. And so you learn to wash a dish as soon as you use it, otherwise it may not be washed for a very long time. You learn to make your bed immediately because there may be no time to do it later. And then you begin to worry regularly, if not constantly, about how to save time. You learn to prepare for the baby's waking as soon as the baby sleeps. You learn to prepare everything hours in advance. Then your conception of time begins to change. The future collapses into the present.

Other Days

There are other days, despite what you have learned about saving time, and preparing ahead, when something in you relaxes, or you are simply tired. You do not mind if the house is untidy. You do not mind if you do nothing but care for the baby. You do not mind if time goes by while you lie in the hammock and read a magazine.

Why He Smiles

He looks at a window with serious interest. He looks at a painting and smiles. It is hard to know what that smile means. Is he pleased by the painting? Is the painting funny to him? No, soon you understand that he smiles at the painting for the same reason he smiles at you: because the painting is looking at him.

A Problem of Balance

A problem of balance: if he yawns, he falls over backward.

Moving Forward

You worry about moving forward, or about the difference between moving forward and staying in one place. You begin to notice which things have to be done over and over again in one day, and which things have to be done once every day, and which things have to be done every few days, and so on, and all these things only cause you to mark time, stay in one place, rather than move forward, or, rather, keep you from slipping backward, whereas certain other things are done only once. A job to earn money is done only once, a letter is written saying a thing only once and never again, an event is planned that will happen only once, news is received or news passed along only once, and if, in this way, something happens that will happen only once, this day is different from other days, and on this day your life seems to move forward, and it is easier to sit still holding the baby and staring at the wall knowing that on this day, at least, your life has moved forward; there has been a change, however small.

A Small Thing with Another Thing, Even Smaller

Asleep in his carriage, he is woken by a fly.

Patience

You try to understand why on some days you have no patience and on others your patience is limitless and you will stand over him for a long time where he lies on his back waving his arms, kicking his legs, or looking up at the painting on the wall. Why on some days it is limitless and on others, or at other times, late in a day when you have been patient, you cannot bear his crying and want to threaten to put him away in his bed to cry alone if he does not stop crying in your arms, and sometimes you do put him away in his bed to cry alone.

Impatience

You learn about patience. You discover patience. Or you discover how patience extends up to a certain point and then it ends and impatience begins. Or rather, impatience was there all along, underneath a light, surface kind of patience, and at a certain point the light kind of patience wears away and all that's left is the impatience. Then the impatience grows.

Paradox

You begin to understand paradox: lying on the bed next to him, you are deeply interested, watching his face and holding his hands, and yet at the same time you are deeply bored, wishing you were somewhere else doing something else.

Regression

Although he is at such an early stage in his development, he regresses, when he is hungry or tired, to an earlier stage, still, of noncommunication, self-absorption, and spastic motion.

Between Human and Animal

How he is somewhere between human and animal. While he can't see well, while he looks blindly toward the brightest light, and can't see you, or can't see your features but more clearly the edge of your face, the edge of your head; and while his movements are more chaotic; and while he is more subject to the needs of his body, and can't be distracted, by intellectual curiosity, from his hunger or loneliness or exhaustion, then he seems to you more animal than human.

How Parts of Him Are Not Connected

He does not know what his hand is doing: it curls around the iron rod of your chair and holds it fast. Then, while he is looking elsewhere, it curls around the narrow black foot of a strange frog.

Admiration

He is filled with such courage, goodwill, curiosity, and self-reliance that you admire him for it. But then you realize he was born with these qualities: now what do you do with your admiration?

Responsibility

How responsible he is, to the limits of his capacity, for his own body, for his own safety. He holds his breath when a cloth covers his face. He widens his eyes in the dark. When he loses his balance, his hands curl around whatever comes under them, and he clutches the stuff of your shirt.

Within His Limits

How he is curious, to the limits of his understanding; how he attempts to approach what arouses his curiosity, to the limits of his motion; how confident he is, to the limits of his knowledge; how masterful he is, to the limits of his competence; how he derives satisfaction from another face before him, to the limits of his attention; how he asserts his needs, to the limits of his force.

The Child
by Ali Smith

I went to Waitrose as usual in my lunchbreak to get
the weekly stuff. I left my trolley by the vegetables and
went to find bouquet garni for the soup. But when I
came back to the vegetables again I couldn't find my
trolley. It seemed to have been moved. In its place was
someone else's shopping trolley, with a child sitting
in its little child seat, its fat little legs through the
leg-places.

Then I glanced into the trolley in which the child
was sitting and saw in there the few things I'd already
picked up: the three bags of oranges, the apricots, the
organic apples, the folded copy of the *Guardian* and the
tub of kalamata olives. They were definitely my things.
It was definitely my trolley.

The child in it was blond and curly-haired, very
fair-skinned and flushed, big-cheeked like a cupid or a
chub-fingered angel on a Christmas card, a child out of
an old-fashioned English children's book, the kind of
book where they wear sunhats to stop them getting
sunstroke all the post-war summer. This child was

wearing a little blue tracksuit with a hood and blue shoes, and was quite clean, though a little crusty around the nose. Its lips were very pink and perfectly bow-shaped; its eyes were blue and clear and blank. It was an almost embarrassingly beautiful child.

Hello, I said. Where's your mother?

The child looked at me blankly.

I stood next to the potatoes and waited for a while. There were people shopping all round. One of them had clearly placed this child in my trolley and when he or she came to push the trolley away I could explain these were my things and we could swap trolleys or whatever and laugh about it and I could get on with my shopping as usual.

I stood for five minutes or so. After five minutes I wheeled the child in the trolley to the Customer Services desk.

I think someone somewhere may be looking for this, I said to the woman behind the desk, who was busy on a computer.

Looking for what, Madam? she said.

I presume you've had someone losing their mind over losing him, I said. I think it's a him. Blue for a boy, etc.

The Customer Services woman was called Marilyn Monroe. It said so on her namebadge.

Quite a name, I said, pointing to the badge.

I'm sorry? she said.

Your name, I said. You know. Monroe. Marilyn.

Yes, she said. That's my name.

She narrowed her eyes at me as if I sounded dangerously foreign to her.

How exactly can I help you? she said in a singsong voice.

Well, as I say, this child, I said.

What a lovely boy! she said. He's very like his mum.

Well, I wouldn't know, I said. He's not mine.

Oh, she said. She looked offended. But he's so like you. Aren't you? Aren't you, darling? Aren't you, sweetheart?

She waved the curly red wire attached to her key ring at the child, who watched it swing inches away from his face, nonplussed. I couldn't imagine what she meant. The child looked nothing like me at all.

No, I said. I went round the corner to get something and when I got back to my trolley he was there, in it.

Oh, she said. She looked very surprised. We've had no reports of a missing child, she said.

She pressed some buttons on an intercom thing.

Hello? she said. It's Marilyn on Customers. Good thanks, how are you? Anything up there on a missing child? No? Nothing on a child? Missing, or lost? Lady here claims she's found one.

She put the intercom down. No Madam, I'm afraid nobody's reported any child that's lost or missing, she said.

A small crowd had gathered behind us. He's adorable, one woman said. Is he your first?

He's not mine, I said.

How old is he? another said.

I don't know, I said.

You don't? she said. She looked shocked.

Aw, he's lovely, an old man, who seemed rather too poor a person to be shopping in Waitrose, said.

He got a fifty pence piece out of his pocket, held it up to me and said: Here you are. A piece of silver for good luck.

He tucked it into the child's shoe.

I wouldn't do that, Marilyn Monroe said. He'll get it out of there and swallow it and choke on it.

He'll never get it out of there, the old man said. Will you? You're a lovely boy. He's a lovely boy, he is. What's your name? What's his name? I bet you're like your dad. Is he like his dad, is he?

I've no idea, I said.

No idea! the old man said. Such a lovely boy! What a thing for his mum to say!

No, I said. Really. He's nothing to do with me, he's not mine. I just found him, in my trolley, when I came back with the—

At this point the child sitting in the trolley looked at me, raised his little fat arms in the air at me and said, straight at me: Mammuum.

Everybody in the little circle of baby admirers looked at me. Some of them looked knowing and sly. One or two nodded at each other.

The child did it again. It reached its arms, almost as if to pull itself up out of the trolley seat and lunge straight at me through the air.

Mummaam, it said.

The woman called Marilyn Monroe picked up her intercom again and spoke into it. Meanwhile the child had started to cry. It screamed and bawled. It shouted its word for mother at me over and over again and shook the trolley with its shouting.

Give him your car keys, a lady said. They love to play with car keys.

Bewildered, I gave the child my keys. It threw them to the ground and screamed all the more.

Lift him out, a woman in a Chanel suit said. He just wants a little cuddle.

It's not my child, I explained again. I've never seen it before in my life.

Here, she said.

She had pulled the child out of the wire basket of the trolley seat, holding it at arm's length so her little suit wouldn't get smeared. It screamed even more as its

53

legs came out of the wire seat, its face got redder and redder and the whole shop resounded with the screaming. I was embarrassed. I felt peculiarly responsible. I'm so sorry, I said to the people round me. The Chanel woman shoved the child hard into my arms.

Immediately it put its arms round me and quietened to fretful cooing.

Jesus Christ, I said, because I had never felt so powerful in all my life.

The crowd round us made knowing noises. See? a woman said. I nodded.

There, the old man said. That'll always do it. You don't need to be scared, love.

Such a pretty child, a passing woman said. The first three years are a nightmare, another said, wheeling her trolley past me towards the fine wines. Yes, Marilyn Monroe was saying into the intercom. Claiming it wasn't. Hers. But I think it's all right now. Isn't it Madam? All right now? Madam?

Yes, I said through a mouthful of the child's blond hair.

Go on home, love, the old man said. Give him his supper and he'll be right as rain.

Teething, a woman ten years younger than me said. She shook her head; she was a veteran. It can drive you crazy, she said, but it's not forever. Don't worry. Go home now and have a nice cup of herb tea and it'll all settle down, he'll be asleep as soon as you know it.

Yes, I said. Thanks very much. What a day.

A couple of women gave me encouraging smiles, one patted me on the arm. The old man patted me on the back, squeezed the child's foot inside its shoe. Fifty pence, he said. That used to be ten shillings. Long before your time, little soldier. Used to buy a week's worth of food, ten shillings did. In the old days, eh? Ah well, some things change and some others never do. Eh? Eh Mum?

Yes. Ha ha. Don't I know it, I said, shaking my head.

*

I carried the child out into the car park. It weighed a ton.

I thought about leaving it right there in the car park behind the recycling bins, where it couldn't do too much damage to itself and someone would easily find it before it starved or anything. But I knew that if I did this the people in the store would remember me and track me down after all the fuss we'd just had. So I laid it on the back seat of the car, buckled it in with one of the seatbelts and the blanket off the back window, and got in the front. I started the engine.

I would drive it out of town to one of the villages, I decided, and leave it there, on a doorstep or outside a shop or something, when no-one was looking, where someone else would report it found and its real parents or whoever had lost it would be able to claim it back. I would have to leave it somewhere without being seen, though, so no one would think I was abandoning it.

Or I could simply take it straight to the police. But then I would be further implicated. Maybe the police would think I had stolen the child, especially now that I had left the supermarket openly carrying it as if it were mine after all.

I looked at my watch. I was already late for work.

I cruised out past the garden centre and towards the motorway and decided I'd turn left at the first signpost and deposit it in the first quiet, safe, vaguely peopled place I found, then race back into town. I stayed in the inside lane and watched for village signs.

You're a really rubbish driver, a voice said from the back of the car. I could do better than that, and I can't even drive. Are you for instance representative of all women drivers, or is it just you among all women who's so rubbish at driving?

It was the child speaking. But it spoke with so surprisingly charming a little voice that it made me want to laugh, a voice as young and clear as a series of ringing bells arranged into a pretty melody. It said the complicated words, representative and for instance, with an innocence that sounded ancient, centuries old, and at the same time as if it had only just discovered their meaning and was trying out their usage and I was privileged to be present when it did.

I slewed the car over to the side of the motorway, switched the engine off and leaned over the front seat into the back. The child still lay there helpless, rolled up in the tartan blanket, held in place by it inside the seat-belt. It didn't look old enough to be able to speak. It looked barely a year old.

It's terrible. Asylum seekers come here and take all our jobs and all our benefits, it said preternaturally, sweetly. They should all be sent back to where they come from.

There was a slight endearing lisp on the "s" sounds in the words asylum and seekers and jobs and benefits and sent.

What? I said.

Can't you hear? Cloth in your ears? it said. The real terrorists are people who aren't properly English. They will sneak into football stadiums and blow up innocent Christian people supporting innocent English teams.

The words slipped out of its ruby-red mouth. I could just see the glint of its little coming-through teeth.

It said: The pound is our rightful heritage. We

deserve our heritage. Women shouldn't work if they're going to have babies. Women shouldn't work at all. It's not the natural order of things. And as for gay weddings. Don't make me laugh.

Then it laughed, blondly, beautifully, as if only for me. Its big blue eyes were open and looking straight up at me as if I were the most delightful thing it had ever seen.

I was enchanted. I laughed back.

From nowhere a black cloud crossed the sun over its face, it screwed up its eyes and kicked its legs, waved its one free arm around outside the blanket, its hand clenched in a tiny fist, and began to bawl and wail.

It's hungry, I thought, and my hand went down to my shirt and before I knew what I was doing I was unbuttoning it, getting myself out, and planning how to ensure the child's later enrolment in one of the area's better secondary schools.

*

I turned the car around and headed for home. I had decided to keep the beautiful child. I would feed it. I would love it. The neighbours would be amazed that I had hidden a pregnancy from them so well, and everyone would agree that the child was the most beautiful child ever to grace our street. My father would dandle the child on his knee. About time too, he'd say. I thought you were never going to make me a grandfather. Now I can die happy.

The beautiful child's melodious voice, in its pure RP pronunciation, the pronunciation of a child who's already been to an excellent public school and learned how exactly to speak, broke in on my dream.

Why do women wear white on their wedding day? it asked from the back of the car.

What do you mean? I said.

Why do women wear white on their wedding day? it said again.

Because white signifies purity, I said. Because it signifies—

To match the stove and the fridge when they get home, the child interrupted. An Englishman, an Irishman, a Chineseman and a Jew are all in an aeroplane flying over the Atlantic.

What? I said.

What's the difference between a pussy and a cunt? the child said in its innocent pealing voice.

Language! please! I said.

I bought my mother-in-law a chair, but she refused to plug it in, the child said. I wouldn't say my mother-in-law is fat, but we had to stop buying her Malcolm X t-shirts because helicopters kept trying to land on her.

I hadn't heard a fat mother-in-law joke for more than twenty years. I laughed. I couldn't not.

Why did they send premenstrual women into the desert to fight the Iraqis? Because they can retain water for four days. What do you call a Pakistani with a paper bag over his head?

Right, I said. That's it. That's as far as I go.

I braked the car and stopped dead on the inside lane. Cars squealed and roared past us with their drivers leaning on their horns and shaking their fists. I switched on the hazard lights. The child sighed.

You're so politically correct, it said behind me, charmingly. And a terrible driver. How do you make a woman blind? Put a windscreen in front of her.

Ha ha, I said. That's an old one.

I took the B roads and drove to the middle of a dense wood. I opened the back door of the car and bundled the beautiful blond child out. I locked the car. I carried the child for half a mile or so until I found a sheltered spot, where I left it in the tartan blanket under the trees.

I've been here before, you know, the child told me. S'not my first time.

Goodbye, I said. I hope wild animals find you and raise you well.

I drove home.

But all that night I couldn't stop thinking about the

helpless child in the woods, in the cold, with nothing to eat and nobody knowing it was there.

I got up at 4 am and wandered round my bedroom. Sick with worry, I drove back out to the wood road, stopped the car in exactly the same place and walked the half-mile back into the trees.

There was the child, still there, still wrapped in the tartan travel rug.

You took your time, it said. I'm fine, thanks for asking. I knew you'd be back. You can't resist me.

I put it in the back seat of the car again.

Here we go again. Where to now? the child said.

Guess, I said.

Can we go somewhere with broadband so I can look up some internet porn? the beautiful child said, beautifully.

I drove to the next city and pulled into the first supermarket car park I passed. It was 6.45 am and it was open.

Ooh, the child said. My first 24-hour Tesco's. I've had an Asda and a Sainsbury's but I've not been to a Tesco's before.

I pulled the brim of my hat down over my eyes to evade being identifiable on closed circuit and carried the tartan bundle in through the out doors when two other people were leaving. The supermarket was very quiet, but there were one or two people shopping. I found a trolley, half-full of good things, French butter, Italian olive oil, a folded new copy of the *Guardian*, left standing in the biscuits aisle, and emptied the child into it out of the blanket, slipping his pretty little legs in through the gaps in the opened child seat.

There you go, I said. Good luck. All the best. I hope you get what you need.

I know what you need all right, the child whispered after me, but quietly, in case anybody should hear. Psst, he hissed. What do you call a woman with two brain cells? Pregnant! Why were shopping trolleys invented? To teach women to walk on their hind legs!

Then he laughed his charming peal of a pure childish laugh and I slipped away out of the aisle and out of the doors past the shopgirls cutting open the plastic binding on the morning's new tabloids and arranging them on the newspaper shelves, and out of the supermarket, back to my car, and out of the car park, while all over England the bells rang out in the morning churches and the British birdsong welcomed the new day, God in his heaven, and all being right with the world.

Café Society

by Helen Simpson

Two shattered women and a bright-eyed child have just sat down at the window table in the café. Both women hope to talk, for their minds to meet; at the same time they are aware that the odds against this happening are about fifty to one. Still they have decided to back that dark horse Intimacy, somewhere out there muffledly galloping. They order coffee, and toast for the boy, who seizes a teaspoon and starts to bash away at the cracked ice marbling of the formica table.

'No, Ben,' says his mother, prising the spoon from his fingers and diverting his attention to the basket of sugar sachets. She flings discreet glances at the surrounding tables, gauging the degrees of irritability of those nearest. There are several other places they could have chosen, but this sandwich bar is where they came.

They might have gone to McDonald's, so cheap and tolerant, packed with flat light and fat smells and unofficial crêche clamour. There they could have slumped like the old punchbags they are while Ben screeched and flew around with the other children. McDonald's is essentially a wordless experience, though, and they both want to see if they can for a wonder exchange some words. Then there is Pete's Café on the main road, a lovely steamy unbuttoned room where men sit in their work clothes in a friendly fug of bonhomie and banter, smoking, stirring silver streams of sugar into mugs of bright brown tea. But it would not be fair to take this child in there and spoil that Edenic all-day-breakfast fun. It would take the insensitivity of an ox. Unthinkable.

Here is all right. They get all sorts here. Here is used to women walking in with that look on their faces – 'What hit me?' Even now there is a confused-looking specimen up there ordering a decaffitated coffee, takeaway, at the counter.

'Every now and then I think *I* might give it up, see if that helps,' says Frances. 'Caffeine. But then I reckon it's just a drop in the ocean.'

Ben rocks backwards in his chair a few times, seeing how far he can go. He is making a resonant zooming noise behind his teeth, but not very loudly yet. Sally keeps her baggy eye on him and says, 'Sometimes I think I'm just pathetic but then other times I think, I'm not a tank.'

'Cannonfodder,' observes Frances.

'It's all right if you're the sort who can manage on four hours,' says Sally. 'Churchill. Thatcher. Bugger.'

Ben, having tipped his chair to the point of no return, carries on down towards the floor in slow motion. Frances dives in and with quiet skill prevents infant skull from hitting lino-clad concrete.

'Reflexes,' says Sally gratefully. 'Shot to pieces.'

She clasps the shaken child to her coat with absent fervour. He is drawing breath for a blare of delayed shock when the arrival of the toast deflects him.

'The camel's back,' says Sally obscurely.

'Not funny,' comments Frances, who understands that she is referring to sleep, or its absence.

Ben takes the buttery knife from the side of his plate and waves it in the air, then drops it onto his mother's coat sleeve. From there it falls to her lap and then, noisily, to the floor. She dabs at the butter stains with a tissue and bangs her forehead as she reaches beneath the table for the knife. Ben laughs and sand-papers his chin with a square of toast.

This woman Sally has a drinker's face, but her lustreless grey skin and saurian eye come not from alcohol but from prolonged lack of sleep.

As a former research student it has often occurred to her that a medical or sociology post-graduate might profitably study the phenomenon in society of a large number of professional women in their thirties suffering from exhaustion. Her third child, this bouncing boy, has woken at least four times a night since he was born. Most mornings he won't go back to sleep after five, so she has him in with her jumping and playing and singing. She hasn't shared a bedroom with her husband for eighteen months now. She'd carried on full-time through the first and second. They slept. Luck of the draw. Yes of course she has talked to her health visitor about this, she has taken the boy to a sleep clinic, she has rung Cry-sis and listened to unseen mothers in the same foundering boat. The health visitor booked her into a sleep counselling course which involved her taking an afternoon every week off work, driving an hour's round trip on the North Circular, only to listen to some well-meaning woman tell her what damage this sleep pattern was causing to the family unit, to her health, to her marriage, to the boy's less demanding siblings. Well she knew all that anyway, didn't she? After the third session she said, what's the point? Not every problem has a solution, she decided, and here it is obviously a brutally simple question of survival, of whether she cracks before he starts sleeping through. It's years now.

These thoughts flash through her mind, vivid and open, but must remain unspoken as Ben's presence precludes anything much in the way of communication beyond blinking in Morse. The few words she has exchanged with this woman Frances, known only by sight after all from the nursery school queue, are the merest tips of icebergs. Such thoughts are dangerous to articulate anyway, bringing up into the air what has been submerged. Nearly all faces close in censorship at the merest hint of such talk. Put up and shut up is the rule, except with fellow mothers. Even then it can be taken as letting the side down. She yawns uncontrollably so that her eyes water, leaving her with the face of a bloodhound.

From her handbag this tired woman Sally takes a pad and felt tips and places them in front of her son Ben, who is rolling his eyes and braying like a donkey.

'Shush Ben,' she says. 'You're not a donkey.'

He looks at her with beautiful affectless eyes. He sucks in air and starts up a series of guttural snorts.

'You're not a piggy, Ben, stop it,' says Sally.

'Piggy,' says Ben, laughing with lunatic fervour.

'They were brilliant at work, they bent over backwards,' says Sally, rapidly, anyway. 'It was me that resigned, I thought it wasn't fair on them. I was going into work for a rest. Ben!'

'That's hard,' says Frances, watching as Sally straightens the boy in his chair and tries to engage him in colouring a picture of a rabbit in police uniform.

'Do you work then?' asks Sally, filling in one long furry ear with pink.

'Yes. No,' says Frances. 'I shouldn't be here! You know, round the edges at the moment. I mean, I must.

I have. Always. Unthinkable! But, erm. You know. Freelance at the moment.'

Ben pushes the paper away from him and grasps at a handful of felt tips. He throws them against the window and cheers at the clatter they make on impact.

'No, Ben!' growls Sally through clenched teeth. 'Naughty.'

The two women grovel under the table picking up pens. Ben throws a few more after them.

What Frances would have said had there been a quiet patch of more than five seconds, was, that she had worked full-time all through the babyhood of her first child, Emma, and also until her second, Rose, was three, as well as running the domestic circus, functioning as the beating heart of the family while deferring to the demands of her partner's job in that it was always her rather than him who took a day off sick when one of the girls sprained a wrist or starred in a concert, and her too of course who was responsible for finding, organising and paying for childcare and for the necessary expenditure of countless megavolts of the vicarious emotional and practical energy involved in having someone else look after your babies while you are outside the house all day, all the deeply unrestful habits of vigilance masquerading as 'every confidence' in the nanny who would, perfectly reasonably, really rather be an aerobics instructor working on Legs Tums 'n' Bums.

Then there was one childcare-based strappado too many; and she cracked. After all those years. She had come home unexpectedly in the afternoon to find the woman fast asleep on the sofa, clubbed out as she later put it, while Emma and Rose played on the stairs with needles and matches or some such. Could be worse, her sensible woman-in-the-workplace voice said; she's young, she likes a good time and why shouldn't she; nothing happened, did it? To hell with that, her mother-in-the-house voice said; I could be the one on the sofa rather than out there busting a gut and barely breaking even.

She needed work, she loved work, she was educated for it. Didn't she, Sally, feel the same way? She'd never asked her partner for money; no, they were equals, pulling together. Well, work was fabulous while you were there, it was what you had to do before and after work that was the killer. It was good for the girls to see their mother out working in the real world, he said when she talked of feeling torn apart; a role model. There's no need to feel guilty, he would begin, with God-like compassion. It's not guilt, you fool. It's the unwelcome awareness that being daily ripped in half is not good, not even ultimately. I agree with all the reasons. 'I'm sorry, they've got to realise that you are a person in your own right and have work to do.' I couldn't agree more. 'Women have always worked, except for that brief sinister time in the fifties.' Yes. But had they always had to work a ten-hour day at a full hour's commuting distance from their *babies while not showing by a murmur or a flicker what this was doing to them?*

So here she was after all these years 'gone freelance', that coy phrase, cramming a full-time job into their school hours and also the evenings once they'd gone to bed. She had a large envelope of sweets pinned to the wall by the telephone so that she could receive work calls to the noise of lollipop-sucking rather than shrilling and howls. And now, of course, she had no sick pay, paid holiday, pension or maternity leave should she be so foolish as to find herself pregnant again. Just as the Welfare State she'd been raised to lean on was packing up.

Unfortunately not one word of this makes it into the light of day, as Ben is creating.

'It was more fun at work,' Frances bursts out, watching Sally wipe the child's buttery jawline with another of the inexhaustible supply of tissues from her bag. 'You get some *respect* at work.'

'My last childminder,' says Sally. She flinches.

'Snap,' says Frances.

The two women sip their powerless cappuccinos.

'In a couple of years' time, when this one starts school,' says Sally, 'I could probably get back, get by with an au pair in term-time. Someone to collect them from school, get their tea. But then there's the holidays.'

'Very long, the holidays,' agrees Frances.

'Not fair on the poor girl,' says Sally. 'Not when she doesn't speak English. Now if it was just Leo he'd be fine,' she continues, off on another tack, thinking aloud about her two eldest children. 'But Gemma is different.'

The child Ben slides off his chair and runs over to the glass-fronted display of sandwich fillings, the metal trays of damp cheese, dead ham and tired old tuna mixed with sweetcorn kernels. He starts to hit the glass with the flat of his hand. There is a collective intake of breath and everyone turns to stare. As she lurches over to apologise and expostulate, Sally's mind continues to follow her train of thought, silently addressing Frances even if all that Frances can see of her is a bumbling, clucking blur.

Children are all different, Sally thinks on, and they are different from birth. Her own son Leo has a robust nature, a level temperament and the valuable ability to amuse himself, which is what makes him so easy to care for. He has smilingly greeted more than half a dozen childminders in his time, and waved them goodbye with equal cheeriness. Gemma, however, was born more anxious, less spirited. She cries easily and when her mother used to leave for work would abandon herself to despair. She is crushingly jealous of this youngest child Ben. She wants to sit on Sally's lap all the time when she is there, and nags and whines like a neglected wife, and clings so hard that all around are uncomfortably filled with irritation. She has formed fervid attachments to the aforementioned childminders, and has wept bitterly at their various departures. Well, Gemma may thrive better now her mother is at home, or she may not; the same could be said of her mother. Time will tell, but by then of course it will be then and not now, and Sally will be unemployable whichever way it has turned out.

'Oof', grunts Sally, returning with her son, who leaps within her arms like a young dolphin. She sits him firmly on his chair again.

'My neighbour's au pair wrote their car off last week,' says Frances. 'Nobody hurt, luckily.'

They both shudder.

'We're so lucky,' they agree, po-faced, glum, gazing at zany Ben as he stabs holes into the police rabbit with a sharp red pen. Sally yawns uncontrollably, then Frances starts up where she leaves off.

After all, they're getting nowhere fast.

An elderly woman pauses as she edges past their table on the way to the till. She cocks her head on one side and smiles brightly at Ben, whose mouth drops open. He stares at her, transfixed, with the expression of a seraph who has understood the mystery of the sixth pair of wings. His mother Sally knows that he is in fact temporarily dumbstruck by the woman's tremendous wart, which sits at the corner of her mouth with several black hairs sprouting from it.

'What a handsome little fellow,' says the woman fondly. 'Make the most of it, dear,' she continues, smiling at Sally. 'It goes so fast.' Sally tenses as she smiles brightly back, willing her son not to produce one of his devastating monosyllables. Surely he does not know the word for wart yet.

'Such a short time,' repeats the woman, damp-eyed.

Well, not really, thinks Frances. Sometimes it takes an hour to go a hundred yards. Now she knows what she knows she puts it at three and a half years per child, the time spent exhausted, absorbed, used up; and, what's more, if not, then something's wrong. That's a whole decade if you have three! This is accurate, wouldn't you agree, she wants to ask Sally; this is surely true for all but those women with Olympic physical stamina, cast-iron immune systems, steel-clad nerves and sensitivities. Extraordinary women; heroines, in fact. But what about the strugglers? The ordinary mother strugglers? Why do they educate us, Sally, only to make it so hard for us to work afterwards? Why don't they insist on hysterectomies for girls who want further education and have done with it? Of course none of this will get said. There is simply no airspace.

Ben's eyes have sharpened and focused on his admirer's huge side-of-the-mouth wart.

'Witch,' he says, loud and distinct.

'Ben,' says Sally. She looks ready to cry, and so does the older woman, who smiles with a hurt face and says, 'Don't worry, dear, he didn't mean anything,' and moves off.

'WITCH', shouts Ben, following her with his eyes.

At this point, Sally and Frances give up. With a scraping of chairs and a flailing of coats, they wordlessly heave themselves and Ben and his paraphernalia up to the counter, and pay, and go. They won't try that again in a hurry. They smile briefly at each other as they say goodbye, wry and guarded. They have exchanged little more than two hundred words inside this hour, and how much friendship can you base on that?

After all, it's important to put up a decent apologia for your life; well, it is to other people, mostly; to come up with a convincing defence, to argue your corner. It's nothing but healthy, the way the sanguine mind does leap around looking for the advantages of any new shift in situation. And if you can't, or won't, you will be shunned. You will appear to be a whiner, or a malcontent. Frances knows this, and so does Sally.

Even so they pause and turn and give each other a brief, gruff, foolish hug, with the child safely sandwiched between them.

Foetus

by Tabitha Siklos

After sex that night, which was at best perfunctory, I lay on my back on top of the duvet with my knees drawn up to my chest, like I'd seen Maude do in *The Big Lebowski*. Owen was in the bathroom and I could tell from the sporadic muffled yelps that he was tweezing his nose hair.

'Gravity,' I said aloud. I'd read about gravity-assisted conception, how to give the swimmers a better chance. Owen was the one who cooed over babies, so I assumed he would applaud my initiative.

I was right. Three weeks later, I waited nervously on a deckchair in our small garden, while Owen checked the pregnancy test. One blue line meant no hCG hormone, no baby. Two blue lines meant baby. Of course it was two. I knew even before Owen burst through the patio doors, holding the pee-stick triumphantly in the air, a wide grin on his face. I just knew. I stood up and we gripped each other tightly.

'This moment,' he said, to me, to the cluster of cells in my uterus, 'this moment we will remember forever.'

Owen knelt to kiss my stomach and when he raised his face to me there was a look in his eyes that I hadn't seen before. It may have been wonder. Or excitement. Or something else.

Week 12

When I arrived home after work, Owen was in the narrow galley kitchen rinsing salad with filtered water and blackening two tuna steaks on a griddle.

'To get rid of the bugs,' he said, as he served up pieces of desiccated fish with a side of damp lettuce. I was finally hungry again and could have murdered a rare steak with blue cheese sauce, but I guessed Owen would rather I went hungry than let me eat bloodied meat and unpasteurised cheese. He poured a glass of wine and a glass of milk and we sat down at the small table.

'I checked the book today,' he said. He'd spent the last few weeks reading *What to Expect When You're Expecting* and regaling me with facts about the developments in my womb. He particularly liked the size comparisons with fruit. We'd been through raspberry, green olive and prune.

'Oh yes?' I stared at the blood red poppy his mother had crocheted, pinned to the front of his jumper.

'The baby is now the size of a plum. Isn't that amazing? It's such a miracle.'

'It's hard to believe that there's a real baby in here.' I gestured to my still-flat stomach and eyed the wine. Owen looked over to the grainy black and white scan photo stuck to the fridge with a magnet in the shape of the Golden Gate Bridge, and smiled. I sipped my milk.

Week 20

I was laid out on the sofa watching *The X Factor* final, when Owen came to sit next to me.

'I've got a little gift for you,' he said. An early Christmas present that he wanted us to open together. He went to get a small package from the spare room and cupped the brown paper parcel in both hands as he presented it to me. It was about the size of a large piece of fruit. I started to feel queasy. He had that look again so I attempted to arrange my face in a smile of gratitude when I saw what lurked inside. I failed. Instead, I grimaced and said, 'What the fuck is that?'

'It's a foetus doll.'

'A what?'

An inert soft-limbed object lay in my lap, naked and hairless. Its moulded plastic face had a little stub nose, pursed pink lips and brown eyelashes over its closed eyes. Owen carefully took the thing from me and lifted it upright. The eyes snapped open. In the low lighting of the living room, two dark eyes stared vacantly into mine.

'I gave them the scan photo and they transposed it onto her face.' I didn't say anything. On the television, Little Mix were singing their cover of 'Silent Night'. Owen said that he'd ordered dark brown eyes, like mine.

'You said you couldn't picture having a baby, so now you, we, can practise. Changing nappies, that sort of thing.' Owen held the thing in his arms. 'It's what she's going to really look like. Can you believe it?'

I stayed up late that night and changed in the bathroom so I didn't wake Owen. I stood naked, looking in the mirror at the small swelling of my belly, my breasts with their visible veins and darkening nipples, the brown line drawn from pubis to tummy button: the *linea negra*. I felt flutters beneath my skin. The quickening, they used to call it, before hormone tests and ultrasounds; evidence that couldn't be dismissed as simply a case of nausea or bloating. Evidence that something was in there, inside.

Owen loved to place his hand flat on my belly and wait for the tremors under the surface, like winged insects flapping and flitting, trying to find their way out. I put on my nightgown, went into our bedroom and bent down over him. I could hear his rhythmic, heavy breathing. I felt the warmth of his face and brushed his curly dark hair with my fingers. Next to his head I felt a smaller head, cold and smooth. I ran my fingertips over the indents of its eye sockets. I pinched its tiny ears lightly. That thing, in our bed.

Week 24

'It's another year now and I'm *still* pregnant.' I perched inelegantly on a bar stool and waited for my third non-alcoholic cocktail of the evening. The barman was pouring a bright orange liquid through a strainer into a tall glass and then piercing pieces of tropical fruit onto a cocktail stick.

'I thought you'd enjoy being part of the baby club,' said Louise.

'It's getting big, though. Too big for Owen's fruit analogies.' I patted my expanding belly. 'I liked imagining it the size of a pineapple, with an orange face and spiky green hair.'

'Shouldn't you be calling it "she" rather than "it"?'

'Yeah, feels strange though, like it's a real person.'

'Er, hello, she's a baby, not a pineapple. Didn't Owen get you a doll to help with all this?'

'Let's not talk about the doll.' I'd found Owen holding the thing the other evening, stroking its cheek and saying 'shhush'. I also noticed that he'd set up the baby monitor on his bedside table. He looked at me guiltily when he saw me staring at it and said, 'just practising.'

The barman placed two drinks on the shiny bar top. Louise and I chinked glasses.

'Let's not talk about either of them,' I said. I slid a chunk of fruit from the stick, put it in my mouth and chewed.

It was late when I got off the train and walked down the long flight of steps out of the station. It had been dark for hours and the road was quiet. A man passed by on the other side of the street, pushing a buggy. He was tall and had a chunky scarf wound around his neck. I could hear the wheels of the buggy turning as I stepped onto the road.

'Owen?' I said. The man didn't turn around. I reached the pavement on the other side, as the man and the buggy disappeared into the shadows of the railway arches. I stared for a minute and then turned and went home. When I opened the front door, the buggy was still in its box in the porch, the knitted scarf from Owen's mother hung from the hatstand. I felt relieved and a bit ridiculous.

As I passed the spare room door on my way up to bed, I paused, turned on the light and went in. John Lewis boxes lay stacked in the corner, the wallpaper was peeling, old green curtains hung thinly from the plastic rail. A pack of newborn nappies lay opened on the changing table. Only the cot in the corner was made up, a clean white sheet stretched over the mattress, a wind-up Peter Rabbit mobile attached to the bars, plush mini bunnies on a carousel. I walked over to the cot and looked in. The thing was lying in the centre under the mobile, wrapped in a pink cellular blanket. Underneath the blanket it was wearing the towelling sleep suit that we'd bought a few weeks earlier. Its eyes were shut.

Week 32

We were late for the NCT class as Owen was fussing over that thing. I waited at the front door, drumming my short fingernails on the wood.

'It's a *doll*, Owen.'

'Yeah,' he said, 'I *know*.' He placed it in the bouncer in front of the TV and flicked to the BabyTV channel.

When we arrived at the church hall at the edge of the tree-lined common, seven other couples were seated on grey plastic chairs arranged in a semicircle. The men looked uncomfortable; the women rubbed their bumps and winced.

The teacher, Denise, who had long blonde hair and a beatified expression, passed around a photo of a woman giving birth outside, in what looked like scrubland, alone. This was supposed to be an example of how women should labour. There were murmurings around the group of how beautiful it was, how natural. One of the women said that this was how she wanted to do it, without drugs or pain relief. Denise nodded her agreement, 'the body knows how,' she enthused. I looked at the photo. The woman was kneeling on the ground, back arched, her face contorted, the tendons in her neck stretched to breaking.

'It looks horrific,' I said. 'Poor woman.'

Denise told us about the signs of early labour: diarrhoea, mucus plugs and the bloody show. Most of the men slumped in their chairs during this part. Denise perked them up with practical instructions on how to time contractions and what to pack in a hospital bag. She told us that our babies would now be covered in lanugo and vernix: downy hair and a greasy, cheesy substance, to stop them pickling in the amniotic sac. That when they were born, their breasts may be engorged, with nipples leaking a thin white liquid named 'witches' milk'.

Owen began to get distracted after lunch; he kept looking at his watch. I thought he was just bored at first; that he'd switched off, like the other men, when Jasmine asked for advice on how to give herself a perineal massage to prevent tearing. But when I looked at him he seemed anxious, panicked even, and I felt a cold dread in the back of my mouth.

He drove home quickly, jaws clenched and silent. I sat beside him clutching the handout showing photos of the varieties of newborn poo, ranging in colour and viscosity. He drove straight into a parking spot outside our home, leaving the back of the car sticking out into the road, and dashed into the house. I sat for a while, remembering what my mother had said about baby poo, my own infant excrement. Like the smell of freshly baked bread, she'd said, playfully, teasingly, knowing she wouldn't be there to help me change a nappy when the time came.

'That seems unlikely,' I said out loud, looking at a picture of a rancid yellow substance and wishing that she was there, that she was here.

As I walked in the door, Owen was in the kitchen bent over the counter, a muslin cloth over his shoulder with that thing perched on top, pinhead eyes staring. He was boiling the kettle and measuring out spoonfuls of formula into a bottle.

'It'll be so much easier when you can breastfeed,' he said, not turning around to look at me.

'I may not bother,' I replied, even though I had fully intended to. He turned around now. 'Oh, you heard what Denise said?'

Yes, I heard what Denise said. That it was important for I.Q., for immunity, that nothing could replace the amber nectar of colostrum. She even claimed to be able to tell by looking at the shape of an adult's chin whether they were breastfed.

'But you weren't breastfed, were you?' I said, looking at his face in profile, which sloped around the jaw area in an unsatisfactory manner. He shook his head, irritated, and took the bottle and the thing upstairs.

Week 36

I nearly walked past my office at work this morning, as there was no name on my door. My desk was clear, apart from the phone and computer. Everyone seemed busy, phones ringing, people running back and forth. Louise passed by a few times and I called her name, but she didn't hear me.

I waddled uncomfortably to her office at lunchtime, conscious that my colleagues eyed the large globe under my tight lycra top with alarm and pressed themselves against the walls of the narrow corridors to let me pass. No-one looked at my face these days. I collapsed into the spare chair in Louise's room with an 'oof,' leant over the desk and squeezed her wrist tightly. I needed to speak to her, about Owen, about home, but I hesitated.

'How are you *feeling?*' she said, leaning forward and patting my clawed hand. No-one asked how I *was* anymore; only how I felt. I adjusted the elasticated waistband of my uncomfortable maternity trousers, leant back in the chair and said I felt fine.

'Fine?' She tilted her large round head to the side, like a planet on an axis, and narrowed her eyes at me. 'How are you feeling about the birth?'

This was something I could talk about. I relaxed. 'Terrified. I mean, how the fuck's it going to get out? It's massive.' I looked down at the body that wasn't my body. Louise laughed.

'Women have been doing this for millennia, I'm told,' she said. The phone rang and she picked it up, mouthing 'sorry' as she put the receiver to her ear. Millennia, yes. But what about when it goes wrong? I'd read the stories, the mothers who died in childbirth, the babies who died, who were still dying daily, hundreds of them. And what about my baby? What if she died? Louise was talking to Marv Chester, my old client. She was holding the receiver in her left hand and writing notes on a lined pad with her right. She wrote 'Trial' at the top of the page and underlined it. Marv used to be my client; I hadn't realised that his case was going to trial. I waited a few minutes more, staring uselessly at the white section of wall over her left shoulder, before I heaved myself from my chair and left the room.

I arrived home from work in daylight. The wisteria was starting to bloom on the climber over the door. Owen was frying minced beef in a casserole dish, wearing a baby sling with that thing in it. He'd started taking the doll to work with him. He introduced it to his colleagues as Feety, since 'foetus doll' was a bit of a mouthful, and the secretaries took it in turns to cuddle it. This is what he'd told me.

I slung my handbag on the floor and leant against the counter.

'I'm getting lots of movement,' I said, easing the backs of my flats from my swollen feet.

'That's a good sign,' he responded, tipping a tin of tomatoes into the dish and stirring.

'Do you want to feel?'

'Sure.' He paused. 'Maybe later, I'll just get this cooked first.'

I stared at the top of the thing's head poking out of the sling. It was wearing a pink hat, the one I'd bought for my baby to wear.

'Give me the doll,' I said.

'Feety.'

'Ok. Fine. Feety. Give me Feety.'

Owen smiled and put down the wooden spoon. He took it carefully from the sling and handed it to me. I held the thing gently, knowing that he was watching me. The doll was ridiculously lightweight. I went to the cupboard, took out eight cans of beans and chopped tomatoes and stacked them up inside the sling.

'Now keep that on for a month,' I said and stomped off upstairs to the loo, ignoring Owen's gasps as I deposited Feety on the kitchen counter.

My limbs ached; I couldn't sleep. I was propped awkwardly on my side, supported by pillows. My ankles were puffed, my thighs lumpy with extra fat and blood, the veins at the top of my legs clumped into large purple pools. The baby inside me stretched and pushed, her feet in my ribcage, her hands pressing the taut skin at the base of my rounded abdomen. It was like the nozzle of a bicycle pump had been inserted in my anus and the piston pumped until the pressure gauge was off the scale.

Owen was breathing deeply. I reached across the many pillows that separated us and shook him. I felt his breath on my face.

'Who is going to remember?' I asked. He murmured and rolled over, his back to me.

'Who is going to remember all the babies who die?' I said, to myself, to my unborn child. When their parents die, there's no-one to remember them. I imagined a pale infant, barely warm, cradled in a mother's arms. In a hospital bed; in a house; outside, alone. It is the same loss. The baby is gone, it doesn't even get a chance.

'And what about you?' I pressed the heel of my hand lightly onto my bump. There was a nudge of a little limb into my palm in response. I smiled. My baby, my daughter, her heart beating inside my body. 'You're going to be just fine,' I said, stroking the place where we had almost touched.

I rose, and despite my weight, padded soundlessly into the nursery. The walls were painted light blue with a border of baby owls, flapping their wings or perched on twigs. Owen had decorated a few weekends ago.

There was a matching blind at the window and packets of cotton wool piled on the changing table. In the cot by the window was Feety.

I stood by the side of the cot and looked down. It was swaddled in a white blanket. The light from the street lamp outside blurred around the edge of the blind and onto its face, illuminating the pale features. Owen had been practising with a thermometer, pretending that Feety had a temperature.

'Are you poorly, Feety?' I whispered. Feety's face was smooth and waxen. I may as well have asked a potato if it had blight. I could have chucked it in the bin, but I didn't. I gave it a little prod in the chest; its head lifted and the plastic eyelids opened.

Week 40

Jasmine sent back her eggs because they were too runny. 'I'm pregnant,' she said, somewhat unnecessarily as she patted her bump of nine months' gestation. We were sitting in a local cafe for brunch, six bumps and two mothers with new babies. The babies arrived hidden under parasols attached to enormous buggies, their mothers laden with massive bags. I tried to keep up with the birth stories and the third trimester woes of the NCT group women, most of whose names I couldn't remember, but I was pre-occupied, distracted.

'I got a contraction when I was in the admissions

queue at Chelsea & Westminster and my waters broke all over the floor . . .'

'My friend's boobs got so hard when her milk came in that her husband had to suck her nipples in the shower to let the milk out.'

'I laboured for 18 hours before I had an epidural. I feel like a failure.'

'I had acupuncture yesterday, to bring on labour. It was totally weird! The guy doing it had dreads, but he was really good.'

'It'd be so special if my baby remembered being in the womb. If that was, like, his first memory.'

'Really?' I said, suddenly interested. 'Suspended upside down in fluid, head pressing against bone, body covered in hair and cheese. Why would you want it to remember that?' Hermione, or someone I thought was called Hermione, paused with her mug of camomile tea held in front of her, her enormous bump adorned with a floral pashmina, what lurked beneath separated from the world by a contraction of muscles, a stretch and tear of skin.

'I think it could be a beautiful experience,' possibly-Hermione countered. 'A point of true connection with my child.'

'Right. Its first sight in the world is of its mother's arsehole.' I felt self-conscious as the bumps and new mothers looked at me, with the tongue on my

A Bigger Bang 2007 tour t-shirt distorted as it stretched over my swollen stomach and breasts. I shrugged. 'Wouldn't you want to forget?'

I stayed in the cafe after the others had left, and then I walked around in the late Spring sunshine for a while, for a long while, until my hips felt like they'd pop out and I wasn't sure where I was anymore. I didn't want to go home, but I was tired. Owen would be there, with the thing. He was there all the time these days; he never seemed to be at work. I resolved to talk to him, to make him engage with me; I'd put it off for too long. I started back in the direction of home. A man overtook me, smoking a cigarette as he walked, the wafts of smoke billowing behind him. I quickened my pace to keep up with him, as much as I could with a skull lodged in my pelvis. I breathed deeply, knowing that Owen would consider this on a par with ramming a knife into my own stomach, but I did it anyway.

The shadows were lengthening in the street as I neared home, and my feet felt as if the arches would collapse from the weight. The cramps started gently at first, but by the time I reached our front door the pain was ramping up. I rested my forehead on the cool oak of the door for a few seconds before I reached for the keys. I slotted the key into the lock. It wouldn't turn. I twisted it back and forth, clutching my stomach with my free hand, but the lock didn't budge. I started to sweat. I felt sticky and put my left hand between my legs. Blood had seeped through my thin cotton trousers. I tried not to panic. Just the bloody show, like Denise said. I banged on the door but no-one came to answer it.

The streetlights were on now. I stood on the pavement and looked up at the nursery window. The blind was down but a lamp was on inside and I could see the outline of a figure through the material, a male figure, cradling something in his arms. The figure was rocking slowly, rhythmically, from side to side. I held onto the door knocker with my right hand as I slid to the doorstep onto my knees and put my bloodied fingers through the letterbox.

'Owen,' I sobbed. 'Owen!' The hallway was dark. A contraction came and I pressed the small of my back to ease the pain. With the next one, a rush of liquid streamed down the inside of my legs and onto the step; not blood but a pale, thin liquid. Amniotic fluid.

The pain intensified; it was blinding, shocking. I was nauseous, wailing, tearing my hair, scrabbling at the door. Someone would hear, someone would see. I felt the excruciating pressure down below, the head of a real baby, ready to tear me in two. Gravity, doing its thing again.

I called Owen's name again in a voice that didn't

sound like mine. Silence, then finally, Owen's voice, deep and melodic, floated down the stairs and through the letterbox. It was the sound of a lullaby, softly sung, 'Hush little baby, don't say a word.' I put my head down onto the concrete doorstep and moaned my despair.

Mother's Son

by Tessa Hadley

Someone told Christine that Alan was going to get married again: the new girl apparently was half his age. Christine didn't think she cared. She hardly ever spoke to Alan these days; there was no need for them to consult together over arrangements for their son, now that Thomas was grown up and made his own arrangements. In fact, after the person told her the news, at a dinner party, Christine forgot it almost at once in the noisy laughter and conversation, and only remembered it again the following afternoon, when she was sitting at home, writing.

She was making notes for a lecture on women novelists and modernism; books by Rhys and Woolf and Bowen were piled all around her, some of them open face down on the table, some of them bristling with torn bits of paper as bookmarks. When she suddenly remembered the news about Alan she lifted her mind from its entanglement in the Paris and Ireland of the twenties and stared around in surprise at her real room in London: tall and white and spacious, with thriving house plants and, filling the wall at one end, a floor-length arched window. The rooms of the flat, where Christine lived alone, were all small – bedroom, bathroom, kitchen – apart from this big one, the centrepiece. Here she worked at a long cherrywood table; when she entertained she pushed all her books and papers to one end and laid places at the other. It was March. Outside the window a bank of dark slate-grey cloud had been piled up by the wind against a lakelike area of silvery-lemon sky, smooth and translucent; the alterations in the light flowed fast, like changing expressions, across the stone housefronts opposite.

Christine's flat was on the second floor; the house was one in a row of houses all with the same phenomenal window and cold north light, built as artists' studios in the 1890s. Some had been renovated and cost the earth, like hers; others were still dilapidated, bohemian, mysterious, the windows draped with rags of patchwork and lace curtains or satin bedspreads. Inside the room, the weather and the light were always intimately present; there were long white curtains at the window but she didn't close them very often. Instead of shutting the drama out, they suggested too eloquently immense presences on the other side. It had been difficult to choose paintings for the walls; in the end Christine had hung a couple of prints of Mondrian drawings. Nothing else had seemed quite still enough.

The doorbell rang, she padded in her stocking feet to the intercom.

—Mum? It's Thomas.

She made them both coffee, hasty – measuring out the grounds, taking down the mugs – in her pleasure at his visit, her eagerness to get back to where her son, her only child, was sprawled in the low-slung white armchair in front of the window. She put milk and sugar on the tray, she was glad she had bought expensive chocolate biscuits. She found an ashtray: no one else was allowed to smoke in her flat. Thomas always for some reason chose that armchair, and then leaned his head back against the headrest so that the ridiculous length of him (he was six foot four) stretched out horizontally, almost as if he were lying flat; he crossed his ankles and squinted frowningly at his shoes.

Today he was wearing his disintegrating old trainers, not the brogues he had for work; his unironed khaki shirt was half in and half out of his trousers. Christine, who hated uniforms, was almost ashamed at how handsome she found him in his obligatory work suit and tie; but she also loved him returned to his crumpled, worn-out old clothes, youth and beauty glowing steadily through them. Thomas was odd-looking, with a crooked nose and a big loose mouth. He hadn't bothered to get his tawny hair cut; his skin flared sensitively where the raw planes of his face were over-growing their childish softness. From under his heavy lids, the green eyes flecked with hazel glanced lazily, like Alan's. If she thought of Alan at all these days (she hadn't seen him more than five or six times in the last twenty years), it was only when Thomas's likeness to him took her by surprise.

—So I hear your father's getting married again?

—Who told you? There was a flicker of solicitous-ness in his expression, in case she minded.

—Someone who knows Laura. Poor Laura.

Laura had been Alan's first wife, the one he was married to all through his affair with Christine, those long years ago. Laura had always made Thomas wel-come in her home, even after Alan strayed a second time, and then a third, and then stayed away perman-ently. Thomas was close to his half-brothers and -sisters, and managed gracefully a whole complex of loyalties.

—I think Laura's OK, Thomas said.—I think she's pretty indifferent these days to what Dad's up to.

This wasn't what the person at the dinner party had told Christine.

—I hear the girl he's marrying is young enough to be his daughter.

Thomas couldn't help his grin: spreading, conspira-torial. He was easily entertained.—You know what he's like.

—Have you met her?

—She's OK. I reckon she knows what she's getting into. But put it this way: I don't think it was her intellectual qualities he fell for. I thought that you might be in college today, he added.—I only came here on the off chance.

—Thursdays I usually work at home. Why aren't you in the office?

—I phoned and told them I was ill. I haven't pulled a sickie for ages. I've got a lot of stuff going round in my head and I wanted some time out to really think about it. And I thought I might stop by to have a bit of a chat about something that's cropped up.

Christine was touched: he rarely came to her to talk about his problems. In fact, there had been almost no problems. He was an affable, sociable boy whose directness was of the easy and not the exacting kind. Thomas heaved himself upright in the chair, so that his knees were jackknifed in front of his face; he stirred two spoons of sugar into his coffee and ate chocolate biscuits.

—Is it about your dad and this wedding?

—God, no. That honestly isn't a big deal. I'm glad for him.

—Work?

He made a face.—And other stuff.

Thomas had finished at Oxford the year before and

had been working as an assistant to a Labour MP, a woman, no one very special. All he did was photocopy and file and send standard answers to constituents' letters, but the idea was that this could lead to bigger and better things, some kind of political career. It was only an idea, being tested. Thomas didn't know whether a political career was what he really wanted. Christine thought he might be too finely constituted, too conscientious for it. On the other hand she was proud of his realism, and that he was thinking unsentimentally about ways to get power and change things.

—I've got myself in a bit of a mess, Thomas said.— With Anna.

—Oh?

He fished his tobacco and rolling papers out of a pocket and used the flat tops of his knees as a table.

—I seem to have got involved with somebody else.

—Oh, Thomas.

He told her about a girl he had met at work. He said that he hadn't liked her at first – he'd thought she was too full of herself. But then they'd had to work on some assignment together and he'd got to know her a lot better. He could talk to her in a way he'd never talked to anyone else. She was very bright. She wasn't good-looking in the way Anna was good-looking.

—She's quite big, he said.—Not fat. Curvy. With this sort of messy black hair. Long.

Thomas's own hair was hanging down across his face as he rolled his cigarette, so Christine couldn't see his expression. She could hear, though, his voice thick with an excitement that she recognised as belonging to the first phase of infatuation, when even speaking about your lover, saying ordinary things about him or her, is a part of desire.

—The worst thing is, he said, shaking his hair back and looking frankly at her.—Well, not the worst thing. But they both have the same name. Not quite the same. She's called Annie.

Christine couldn't help a puff of laughter.

—I know, he said.—Shite, isn't it? He laughed with her.—The two Anns.

—Have you told Anna?

He shook his head.—I thought at first it was just, you know, nothing. Not worth upsetting her about.

—But it's something?

He shrugged and opened his hands at her in a gesture of defencelessness, squinting in the smoke from the roll-up that wagged in his mouth. How was he to know? Nothing like this had ever happened to him before.

Christine felt protective of Anna, although she had sometimes thought her too sweet and dull for Thomas. How clearly she could imagine this new girl: less pretty, overweight, clever, treacherous. These were all the things that she herself had been: she was on her guard at once, as if against a rival.

—She's different, he said.—She's funny; she makes me laugh. She doesn't take everything too seriously.

—And how do you feel about deceiving Anna?

He gulped his coffee. She saw him flooded with shame then, not able to trust himself to speak: an unpractised liar.

—These things happen, she soothed.—We can't pretend they don't. Even if we were good, if we were perfectly and completely chaste, we can't control what happens in our imagination. So being good might only be another kind of lie.

When Christine had begun her affair with Alan, there had been a possibility of his leaving his wife and family. For a while, in fact, he had left, and they had lived together. Thomas was conceived during that time. It had not worked out, they had fought horribly, and Alan had been sick with missing his children. In the end he had taken himself home. Such storms, such storms, there had been in Christine's life then: with Alan, and with others, afterwards. When she longed for her youth, those storms were what she missed, and not the happy times. The excitement of upheaval, a universe open with possibility, the phone calls that changed everything, the conspiratorial consultations with girlfriends, the feverish packing for surprise trips, escaping out of the last thing or rushing to embrace the next. Perhaps Thomas remembered some of those adventures, too: late-night train journeys when he had sat beside her with big sleepless eyes, sucking at his dummy, fingering the precious corner of his blanket, his little red suitcase packed with books and toys.

Later, once he was established at school, she had settled into a steadier routine for his sake. But perhaps now, when he found himself infatuated and intoxicated and behaving badly, at some level of consciousness he'd recognised it as her terrain, and come to her because he thought she would know what he should do next. Perhaps his coming to her with his own crisis was a kind of forgiveness, for those upheavals.

—What about work? she said.

Thomas looked at her vaguely. Work seemed, of course, a straw, in relation to the great conflagration of his passionate life.

—You said there were work issues as well that you were worried about.

—Only the old question. I mean, here I am stuffing envelopes for an MP who voted for the war in Iraq. Should I stay inside the tent pissing out? Perhaps it would be more dignified to get out and do some pissing in.

—Dignified pissing.

—But we've been over all that so many times.

—Only now it's complicated because she's there at work? Annie.

—It would solve everything if I just took off and went away by myself to live in Prague or somewhere. Budapest.

—Leave both of them you mean? Christine said.—Woman trouble, she sighed, making a joke of it.

She was suddenly quite sure that he would, in fact, move abroad for a while, even though he didn't know it yet himself, and it had only popped into his conversation as a joke-possibility. After much confabulation and self-interrogation and any number of painful scenes with his two girls, this was what he would do.

—I'd miss you if you moved to Prague, she said.

—Get a sabbatical. Come out and stay.

She loved having him near her in London. But as soon as she had imagined Prague she knew that it was what she wanted for him: something more than the slick game of opportunity and advancement, a broader and deeper initiation into old sophisticated Europe, into a grown-up life with complications.

—I have to go, Thomas said.

He had looked at his watch three or four times in the last fifteen minutes.

—You're meeting Annie?

—No, he lied.

Though he had made his confession to Christine,

she wasn't even in imagination to follow him to wherever he was meeting his big, dark, clever girl. She was only his mother, after all. It might be Anna's night for Pilates or whatever it was she did. The lovers might have the whole evening ahead of them, after Annie had finished work, to sit in a hidden corner in a pub somewhere, crushing out cigarettes half smoked, going over and over the same broken bits of logic, pressing knees against knees under the table, getting excitedly drunker. Or to go back to her place. All that stuff.

By the time Thomas left, the sky outside Christine's window had changed again. The bank of grey-black had broken up and swallowed the lemon lake; now tousled scraps of cloud tumbled untidily in a brooding light. Christine had another hour to work before she finished for the day and showered and changed; she was meeting a friend for a film – a Bergman screening at the BFI – and a late supper. She picked up her copy of *Good Morning, Midnight*. Her name was on the flyleaf: Christine Logan, Girton College, 1971. She was certain that she had held this same copy in her hands the morning of the day that Thomas was born, in 1980 – not his birthday but the day before, since he wasn't actually born until half past midnight. She had been working on her thesis then, typing up a new chapter to show her supervisor, checking every quotation carefully against her text, when she felt the first pain.

The first pain – the first sign she'd had that Thomas was coming, two weeks before his time – had been like a sharp tiny bell struck as a signal; feeling it had been more like hearing something, a very precise high note, from deep inside her swollen abdomen, which was pressed with some difficulty into the space between her chair and the little rickety desk she worked at. None of the other things that the midwives at the hospital had warned her to expect had happened – the show of bloody mucus, or the waters breaking – only this little bell of pain, so small it was more pleasurable than unpleasant, zinging away from time to time inside her. She knew that she was supposed to delay going into the hospital for as long as she could, so she continued typing, her mind seeming to move at a pitch of high, free clarity between the words of the novel and her own extraordinary circumstance. All this went on in the sitting room of the little cottage she rented from Jesus College in those days, in the Kite in Cambridge. The cottage was gone now, pulled down to make way for new developments.

Once, while she waited, she had got up from the desk and stared at her face in a tarnished old junk-shop mirror she kept propped up on the mantelpiece for the sake of its frame. She thought that only fifty years before, at the time when the Rhys novel was written, she might have stared at herself like this, on the brink of the unknown ordeal, and been justified in wondering whether she would survive it. In the novel, Sasha's baby died. Christine was not afraid, exactly, but she could not imagine what lay in wait for her on the far side of the hours to come. When she was at the hospital for her antenatal appointments, she had sometimes passed new mothers walking out to a waiting car or a taxi, followed by nurses carrying their babies bundled in white shawls. She didn't have friends with babies; she didn't know what it would mean, to be responsible for a white-wrapped bundle of her own.

She had picked up the telephone once or twice to call Alan, but cut herself off before she even finished dialling. Although the plan had always been for him to be there with her at the birth of their child, for the first time the idea of his large presence bothered her: he was a big tall man with a booming voice and a curling salt-and-pepper beard, a historian, a Marxist. I can manage this by myself, she had thought that morning, timing the little bells of pain which began to ring louder and stronger. It was as if she had intuited with the first pang of Thomas's arrival, and quite rightly, that her delighted possession of her son would push apart whatever mechanism it was that had bound her to his father for those years of her youth.

Christine's thesis was on certain women writers of the early twentieth century. She had argued that in their novels and stories they had broken with the conventions deep-buried in the foundations of the fiction tradition: that all good stories end in marriage, and that the essential drive in plot is courtship, bringing men and women together. Katherine Mansfield's *femmes seules* and Woolf's solitaries represented a break that was at least as revolutionary, surely, as Lawrence's and Joyce's iconoclasm. In the late seventies, the automatic gesture of obeisance to feminism had not yet been internalised among academics, and an amused hostility was still the norm. Alan wouldn't read Christine's work then: he said once that he took no interest in the nuances of bourgeois ladies' hypersensibility. She had tolerated this attitude, at least at first; she had even been attracted by it, as if in his contemptuous maleness he were a huge handsome bear whose ferocity she had to take on, and tame, and teach.

When Thomas was four or five years old he had asked her once if he was going to die. She wasn't sure where this exchange had taken place – on a beach perhaps, although not on a summer day. She associated it vaguely with a windy walk across pale pebbles that were awkward underfoot, along the sea's rim of crisp-dried detritus: seaweed, plastic netting, bird bones. Perhaps it was on one of their trips to the Norfolk coast with Alan when he and she were still seeing each other.

She must have been carrying Thomas. She remembered his weight slipping on her hip.

—It's all right, Christine said.—Don't worry about dying. Maybe by the time you grow up they'll have invented some medicine so you won't have to.

She remembered Alan stopping abruptly. Perhaps she put Thomas down then and he went to dabble in the sea-rubbish.

—I can't believe you just said that.

He was laughing, but she thought with certainty at that moment: He hates me. The conviction reverberated like a blow against armour; she tasted blood and she wanted to fight.

—What's wrong with saying it? I used to think that when I was a little girl.

—But it isn't true.

—Of course it's not true. It's something reassuring to keep you going until you're old enough. You know, like Heaven.

—If any adult had ever lied to me about anything so important, when I found out the truth I'd never have forgiven them.

She was shocked at herself, for a moment: she wondered if he was right. Then, recovering, she mocked him.

—But that's just what you're like, isn't it? You love to go around not forgiving people for things. How austere and rigorous it must make you feel. What a little prig of a child you must have been.

He opened his mouth to answer, closed it, and turned to stride away from her down the beach. She hurried raggedly after him, not finished, snatching Thomas up from whatever he was interested in: threading washed-up ring pulls on his fingers or poking a dead gull with a stick. In her memory a wind came whipping up, tearing out her words.

—So what would you have told him, then? If you're so truthful.

He wanted to keep his mouth shut against her but he couldn't resist giving his opinion, beautifully expressed. There had been a time when she would have hung on these words of his devotedly.—I'd tell him that without death life would be formless. That change is the life force.

Christine burst out with a loud snort of laughter.—Well, try that then! Just try it. What d'you think about that, Thomas? Daddy says you have to die, but not to worry. It will give your life a nicer shape.

Thomas gave a rather stagy mew of despair, as if in fact he'd lost interest in the subject, and snuggled his head reproachfully against Christine's lapel. Alan thought Christine encouraged him to be precocious.

He walked away from them now, faster than they could follow, his shoulders in his black greatcoat bowed against the wind, head down, his hair blowing out behind. Then for a while he turned round and walked backwards, facing them, looking at them. Christine couldn't remember if that argument had actually been the end of things, or if they'd made a truce later that afternoon or that night, in whatever hotel or rented cottage they were staying in, and gone on patching things up for a while longer.

The morning after Thomas's visit, Christine was climbing the stairs to her office at the university when someone came running up below her.

—Dr Logan?

Christine paused, resting her pile of books and papers on the banister; someone young with a blonde head lifted to look up at her came around the stairwell with a clatter of heels.

—Dr Logan? Do you mind if I just talk to you for a moment?

Because she was expecting a student with a query about an essay, there was a disconcerting lapse of seconds before Christine registered that the blonde head belonged to Anna, Thomas's girlfriend, whom she'd known for three years. Of course, there was no reason for Anna, who worked in the wardrobe department at

English National Opera, to be on campus: she had never been there before. Also, she had never called Christine Dr Logan.

—Anna, darling, how lovely to see you. Whatever are you doing here? How did you find me?

—I want to talk about Tom.

In one smooth movement, feeling in her bag for her office keys, Christine decided that her first loyalty was to Thomas's confidence. She turned on Anna a look wiped clear of any foreknowledge.

—Is something wrong?

Anna's face was guilelessly open, sorrow stamped on it like a black bootprint. She could not speak until Christine had her door open and they were safely inside. Under the posters and potted plants Christine put the kettle on – Anna nodded an indifferent assent – to make peppermint tea. Anna pressed her palms against her cheeks: her hands were big and pink and sensitive, like her ears, with fingertips reddened from sewing.

—He's seeing someone else.

At least Christine wouldn't pretend not to take her seriously.

—Tell me about it.

—I mean, I don't have any proof. Just the usual silly stuff. Times he's late coming home, things he says he's doing that don't sound quite right. Just something:

like he's all the time slightly impatient with me, but then he's sorry for that and covering it up by being extra nice. I just know the way Tom would be if he were doing it.

—It could be nothing. I know he's the nicest boy in the world, but underneath all that he can be moody.

—I actually thought he might have talked to you. I know he came to see you yesterday. I haven't spoken to anyone else about this.

Anna had always treated Christine with tender respect. Now she scanned her intently with strained-open blue eyes, careless in her desperation. Love, this destroying kind of love, swelled the girl up, gave her a ferocity and an authority that Christine had never seen in her before.

She shook her head sympathetically.—He talked about work.

—He didn't say anything about me that struck you?

—He worries about whether he's doing the right thing, in his job.

—Is that all? Are you sure? I have to know what he's thinking.

—He's bored stuffing envelopes for someone he doesn't believe in.

Anna sighed, frowning impatiently at Christine, or through her: she would know what she was looking for when she found it, and it wasn't this. She wasn't convinced that Christine was telling the whole truth. A pressured moment swayed in the air between them: Anna jostling roughly for more, Christine blandly resisting.

—He did mention wanting to travel in Europe. But I don't know how serious that was.

—You see. I've not heard anything about that. Where in Europe exactly? When? Who with?

—He was probably only talking about a holiday. Budapest, perhaps? He didn't say anything about who with.

—There. You see?

—I suppose I simply took it that he meant alone.

Anna stood up from the swivel office chair and turned to stare out of the window at nothing, below: a nowhere space between the Humanities block and Social Sciences, furnished with a few benches and young trees. She was tall, the same height as Christine, but with a figure that Christine had never had: high full round breasts, a narrow graspable waist, long slender haunches that suggested some graceful running creature, a gazelle. Between her short cut-off top and the absurdly low waistband of her trousers was a long expanse of flawless goosefleshed golden skin, curving into a sweet round rump. The clothes seemed incidental; Anna's young nakedness was in the room between them. With a sharpness almost like longing, Christine was aware of Anna's piercings, even now that her back was turned: in her nose and her belly button, gold rings with little ruby-coloured beads. These young women didn't know what they had. They suffered because they couldn't have Thomas to keep, but they had the struggle over him, the game of pursuit and being pursued, and the sometime possession of him in the flesh. For as long as the thought lasted, that snatched possession felt to Christine like the only thing worth living for: a possibility of joy that was no longer available to the mothers of these children.

Anna turned from the window. Her face was blotched an ugly red with tears.

—What would you do?

—Well, I'd ask him, Christine said at once.—Don't you think that he'll tell you the truth?

—Yes, Anna said bleakly.—I expect he will.

At home Christine prepared an omelette for her supper. She washed lettuce hearts and vine tomatoes; she sliced cucumber and made a vinaigrette. She mashed parsley into a lump of butter with lemon juice, and sautéed a little tinned tuna in a pan with finely chopped shallots. When all this was ready she broke the eggs into a bowl, to beat them. The second egg had gone bad. It felt strange to the touch, the shell weak and scabbed, but even as she registered this it was too late – she had cracked the egg against the side of the bowl and a foul greenish liquid poured out between her fingers, the thin texture of water, not albumen. A stink of putrefaction thrust wildly, rudely, into the kitchen.

She didn't know what to do; she pressed her mouth and nose against her sleeve, not pulling the shell apart any further, not wanting to see inside. The mess was too awful, too violently offensive, to pour down the drain; it would surely come back at her, and perhaps at her neighbours, for hours afterwards. She found an empty peanut-butter jar with a lid, saved for recycling, tipped the whole lot into that, and screwed the lid on, only half allowing herself to look at it. Then she ran downstairs out of her flat to the bins outside, where she buried the jar deep among the rubbish bags.

Upstairs she opened all the windows, even though it was raining, ran water for long minutes down the sink. She bleached the egg bowl and the dishcloth she had used to wipe up the few drops of egg that had spattered on the counter; she washed her hands in the bathroom over and over. Still, every time she put her fingers to her nose she was haunted by the smell. The thought of the rest of her supper nauseated her; she tipped the salad and the tuna into the bin. She knew she was being irrational; she ought to phone a friend and make a joke out of her small disaster, and perhaps go out for a drink and something to eat. Instead she abandoned herself to sulking, lying on her side on the sofa, her hands clasped between her knees. The idea came to her out of nowhere that there would be a last time that she brought anyone home to make love in her bed. It was not yet, it might not be for years, but it would come, even though she might not recognise it until long afterwards.

How could Christine envy Thomas's two girls? Who could want to be one of the two foolish Anns, desperate for him? Or to be Alan, with his beard shaven and his silvery hair clipped close to his skull, hoping to start out on the adventure of passion all over again? How much happier she was, how much less time and energy it took to be Thomas's mother: a relationship founded on one fixed and unalterable truth. Outside her spectacular arched window the wind threw rain in long ragged gusts across the housefronts and tore at the estate agents' signs, setting them flapping in crazy ecstasy. Christine told herself that she was glad she was on this side of the glass, but she lay still on her sofa for a long time, and after a while she turned her back on the view.

Girl

by Jamaica Kincaid

Wash the white clothes on Monday and put them on the stone heap; wash the color clothes on Tuesday and put them on the clothesline to dry; don't walk barehead in the hot sun; cook pumpkin fritters in very hot sweet oil; soak your little cloths right after you take them off; when buying cotton to make yourself a nice blouse, be sure that it doesn't have gum on it, because that way it won't hold up well after a wash; soak salt fish overnight before you cook it; is it true that you sing benna* in Sunday school?; always eat your food in such a way that it won't turn someone else's stomach; on Sundays try to walk like a lady and not like the slut you are so bent on becoming; don't sing benna in Sunday school; you mustn't speak to wharf-rat boys, not even to give directions; don't eat fruits on the street—flies will follow you; *but I don't sing benna on Sundays at all and never in Sunday school;* this is how to sew on a button; this is how to make a

_____
* Calypso songs.

buttonhole for the button you have just sewed on; this is how to hem a dress when you see the hem coming down and so to prevent yourself from looking like the slut I know you are so bent on becoming; this is how you iron your father's khaki shirt so that it doesn't have a crease; this is how you iron your father's khaki pants so that they don't have a crease; this is how you grow okra—far from the house, because okra tree harbors red ants; when you are growing dasheen, make sure it gets plenty of water or else it makes your throat itch when you are eating it; this is how you sweep a corner; this is how you sweep a whole house; this is how you sweep a yard; this is how you smile to someone you don't like very much; this is how you smile to someone you don't like at all; this is how you smile to someone you like completely; this is how you set a table for tea; this is how you set a table for dinner; this is how you set a table for dinner with an important guest; this is how you set a table for lunch; this is how you set a table for breakfast; this is how to behave in the presence of men who don't know you very well, and this way they won't recognize immediately the slut I have warned you against becoming; be sure to wash every day, even if it is with your own spit; don't squat down to play marbles—you are not a boy, you know; don't pick people's flowers—you might catch something; don't throw stones at blackbirds, because it might not be a blackbird at all; this is how to make a bread pudding; this is how to make doukona; this is how to make pepper pot; this is how to make a good medicine for a cold; this is how to make a good medicine to throw away a child before it even becomes a child; this is how to catch a fish; this is how to throw back a fish you don't like, and that way something bad won't fall on you; this is how to bully a man; this is how a man bullies you; this is how to love a man, and if this doesn't work there are other ways, and if they don't work don't feel too bad about giving up; this is how to spit up in the air if you feel like it, and this is how to move quick so that it doesn't fall on you; this is how to make ends meet; always squeeze bread to make sure it's fresh; *but what if the baker won't let me feel the bread?*; you mean to say that after all you are really going to be the kind of woman who the baker won't let near the bread?

Sweetness

by Toni Morrison

It's not my fault. So you can't blame me. I didn't do it and have no idea how it happened. It didn't take more than an hour after they pulled her out from between my legs for me to realize something was wrong. Really wrong. She was so black she scared me. Midnight black, Sudanese black. I'm light-skinned, with good hair, what we call high yellow, and so is Lula Ann's father. Ain't nobody in my family anywhere near that color. Tar is the closest I can think of, yet her hair don't go with the skin. It's different—straight but curly, like the hair on those naked tribes in Australia. You might think she's a throwback, but a throwback to what? You should've seen my grandmother; she passed for white, married a white man, and never said another word to any one of her children. Any letter she got from my mother or my aunts she sent right back, unopened. Finally they got the message of no message and let her be. Almost all mulatto types and quadroons did that back in the day—if they had the right kind of hair, that is. Can you imagine how many white folks have Negro blood hiding in their veins? Guess. Twenty per cent, I heard. My own mother, Lula Mae, could have passed easy, but she chose not to. She told me the price she paid for that decision. When she and my father went to the courthouse to get married, there were two Bibles, and they had to put their hands on the one reserved for Negroes. The other one was for white people's hands. The Bible! Can you beat it? My mother was a house-keeper for a rich white couple. They ate every meal she cooked and insisted she scrub their backs while they sat in the tub, and God knows what other intimate things they made her do, but no touching of the same Bible.

Some of you probably think it's a bad thing to group ourselves according to skin color—the lighter the better—in social clubs, neighborhoods, churches, sororities, even colored schools. But how else can we hold on to a little dignity? How else can we avoid being spit on in a drugstore, elbowed at the bus stop, having to walk in the gutter to let whites have the whole side-walk, being charged a nickel at the grocer's for a paper bag that's free to white shoppers? Let alone all the name-calling. I heard about all of that and much, much more. But because of my mother's skin color she wasn't stopped from trying on hats or using the ladies' room in the department stores. And my father could try on shoes in the front part of the shoe store, not in a back room. Neither one of them would let themselves drink from a "Colored Only" fountain, even if they were dying of thirst.

I hate to say it, but from the very beginning in the maternity ward the baby, Lula Ann, embarrassed me. Her birth skin was pale like all babies', even African ones, but it changed fast. I thought I was going crazy when she turned blue-black right before my eyes. I know I went crazy for a minute, because—just for a few seconds—I held a blanket over her face and pressed. But I couldn't do that, no matter how much I wished she hadn't been born with that terrible color. I even thought of giving her away to an orphanage someplace. But I was scared to be one of those mothers who leave their babies on church steps. Recently, I heard about a couple in Germany, white as snow, who had a dark-skinned baby nobody could explain. Twins, I believe—one white, one colored. But I don't know if it's true. All I know is that, for me, nursing her was like having a pickaninny sucking my teat. I went to bottle-feeding soon as I got home.

My husband, Louis, is a porter, and when he got back off the rails he looked at me like I really was crazy and looked at the baby like she was from the planet Jupiter. He wasn't a cussing man, so when he said, "God damn! What the hell is this?" I knew we were in trouble. That was what did it—what caused the fights between me and him. It broke our marriage to pieces. We had three good years together, but when she was born he blamed me and treated Lula Ann like she was a stranger—more than that, an enemy. He never touched her.

I never did convince him that I ain't never, ever fooled around with another man. He was dead sure I was lying. We argued and argued till I told him her blackness had to be from his own family—not mine. That was when it got worse, so bad he just up and left and I had to look for another, cheaper place to live. I did the best I could. I knew enough not to take her with me when I applied to landlords, so I left her with a teenage cousin to babysit. I didn't take her outside much, anyway, because, when I pushed her in the baby carriage, people would lean down and peek in to say something nice and then give a start or jump back before frowning. That hurt. I could have been the babysitter if our skin colors were reversed. It was hard enough just being a colored woman—even a high-yellow one—trying to rent in a decent part of the city. Back in the nineties, when Lula Ann was born, the law was against discriminating in who you could rent to, but not many landlords paid attention to it. They made up reasons to keep you out. But I got lucky with Mr. Leigh, though I know he upped the rent seven dollars from what he'd advertised, and he had a fit if you were a minute late with the money.

I told her to call me "Sweetness" instead of "Mother" or "Mama." It was safer. Her being that black and having what I think are too thick lips and calling me "Mama" would've confused people. Besides, she has funny-colored eyes, crow black with a blue tint—something witchy about them, too.

So it was just us two for a long while, and I don't have to tell you how hard it is being an abandoned wife. I guess Louis felt a little bit bad after leaving us like that, because a few months later on he found out where I'd moved to and started sending me money once a month, though I never asked him to and didn't go to court to get it. His fifty-dollar money orders and my night job at the hospital got me and Lula Ann off welfare. Which was a good thing. I wish they would stop calling it welfare and go back to the word they used when my mother was a girl. Then it was called "relief." Sounds much better, like it's just a short-term breather while you get yourself together. Besides, those welfare clerks are mean as spit. When finally I got work and didn't need them anymore, I was making more money than they ever did. I guess meanness filled out their skimpy paychecks, which was why they treated us like beggars. Especially when they looked at Lula Ann and then back at me—like I was trying to cheat or something. Things got better but I still had to be careful. Very careful in how I raised her. I had to be strict, very strict. Lula Ann needed to learn how to behave, how to keep her head down and not to make trouble. I don't care how many times she changes her name. Her color is a cross she will always carry. But it's not my fault. It's not my fault. It's not.

Oh, yeah, I feel bad sometimes about how I treated Lula Ann when she was little. But you have to understand: I had to protect her. She didn't know the world. With that skin, there was no point in being tough or sassy, even when you were right. Not in a world where you could be sent to a juvenile lockup for talking back or fighting in school, a world where you'd be the last one hired and the first one fired. She didn't know any of that or how her black skin would scare white people or make them laugh and try to trick her. I once saw a girl nowhere near as dark as Lula Ann who couldn't have been more than ten years old tripped by one of a group of white boys and when she tried to scramble up another one put his foot on her behind and knocked her flat again. Those boys held their stomachs and bent over with laughter. Long after she got away, they were still giggling, so proud of themselves. If I hadn't been watching through the bus window I would have helped her, pulled her away from that white trash. See, if I hadn't trained Lula Ann properly she wouldn't have known to always cross the street and avoid white boys. But the lessons I taught her paid off, and in the end she made me proud as a peacock.

I wasn't a bad mother, you have to know that, but I may have done some hurtful things to my only child because I had to protect her. Had to. All because of skin privileges. At first I couldn't see past all that black to know who she was and just plain love her. But I do. I really do. I think she understands now. I think so.

Last two times I saw her she was, well, striking. Kind of bold and confident. Each time she came to see me, I forgot just how black she really was because she was using it to her advantage in beautiful white clothes.

Taught me a lesson I should have known all along. What you do to children matters. And they might never forget. As soon as she could, she left me all alone in that awful apartment. She got as far away from me as she could: dolled herself up and got a big-time job in California. She don't call or visit anymore. She sends me money and stuff every now and then, but I ain't seen her in I don't know how long.

I prefer this place—Winston House—to those big, expensive nursing homes outside the city. Mine is small, homey, cheaper, with twenty-four-hour nurses and a doctor who comes twice a week. I'm only sixty-three—too young for pasture—but I came down with some creeping bone disease, so good care is vital. The boredom is worse than the weakness or the pain, but the nurses are lovely. One just kissed me on the cheek when I told her I was going to be a grandmother. Her smile and her compliments were fit for someone about to be crowned. I showed her the note on blue paper that I got from Lula Ann—well, she signed it "Bride," but I never pay that any attention. Her words sounded giddy. "Guess what, S. I am so, so happy to pass along this news. I am going to have a baby. I'm too, too thrilled and hope you are, too." I reckon the thrill is about the baby, not its father, because she doesn't mention him at all. I wonder if he is as black as she is. If so, she needn't worry like I did. Things have changed a mite from when I was young. Blue-blacks are all over TV, in fashion magazines, commercials, even starring in movies.

There is no return address on the envelope. So I guess I'm still the bad parent being punished forever till the day I die for the well-intended and, in fact, necessary way I brought her up. I know she hates me. Our relationship is down to her sending me money. I have to say I'm grateful for the cash, because I don't have to beg for extras, like some of the other patients. If I want my own fresh deck of cards for solitaire, I can get it and not need to play with the dirty, worn one in the lounge. And I can buy my special face cream. But I'm not fooled. I know the money she sends is a way to stay away and quiet down the little bit of conscience she's got left.

If I sound irritable, ungrateful, part of it is because underneath is regret. All the little things I didn't do or did wrong. I remember when she had her first period and how I reacted. Or the times I shouted when she stumbled or dropped something. True. I was really upset, even repelled by her black skin when she was born and at first I thought of . . . No. I have to push those memories away—fast. No point. I know I did the best for her under the circumstances. When my husband ran out on us, Lula Ann was a burden. A heavy one, but I bore it well.

Yes, I was tough on her. You bet I was. By the time she turned twelve going on thirteen, I had to be even tougher. She was talking back, refusing to eat what I cooked, primping her hair. When I braided it, she'd go to school and unbraid it. I couldn't let her go bad. I slammed the lid and warned her about the names she'd be called. Still, some of my schooling must have rubbed off. See how she turned out? A rich career girl. Can you beat it?

Now she's pregnant. Good move, Lula Ann. If you think mothering is all cooing, booties, and diapers you're in for a big shock. Big. You and your nameless boyfriend, husband, pickup—whoever—imagine, Oooh! A baby! *Kitchee kitchee koo!*

Listen to me. You are about to find out what it takes, how the world is, how it works, and how it changes when you are a parent.

Good luck, and God help the child.

Of Mothers and Children

by Ngũgĩ wa Thiong'o

Mugumo

Mukami stood at the door: slowly and sorrowfully she turned her head and looked at the hearth. A momentary hesitation. The smouldering fire and the small stool by the fire-side were calling her back. No. She had made up her mind. She must go. With a smooth, oiled upper-garment pulled tightly over her otherwise bare head, and then falling over her slim and youthful shoulders, she plunged into the lone and savage darkness.

All was quiet and a sort of magic pervaded the air. Yet she felt it threatening. She felt awed by the immensity of the darkness – unseeing, unfeeling – that enveloped her. Quickly she moved across the courtyard she knew so well, fearing to make the slightest sound. The courtyard, the four huts that belonged to her *airu*, the silhouette of her man's hut and even her own, seemed to have joined together in one eternal chorus of mute condemnation of her action.

'You are leaving your man. Come back!' they pleaded

in their silence of pitying contempt. Defiantly she crossed the courtyard and took the path that led down to the left gate. Slowly, she opened the gate and then shut it behind her. She stood a moment, and in that second Mukami realized that with the shutting of the gate, she had shut off a part of her existence. Tears were imminent as with a heavy heart she turned her back on her rightful place and began to move.

But where was she going? She did not know and she did not very much care. All she wanted was to escape and go. Go. Go anywhere – Masailand or Ukambani. She wanted to get away from the hearth, the courtyard, the huts and the people, away from everything that reminded her of Muhoroini Ridge and its inhabitants. She would go and never return to him, her hus—No! not her husband, but the man who wanted to kill her, who would have crushed her soul. He could no longer be her husband, though he was the very same man she had so much admired. How she loathed him now.

Thoughts of him flooded her head. Her young married life: Muthoga, her husband, a self-made man with four wives but with a reputation for treating them harshly; her father's reluctance to trust her into his hands and her dogged refusal to listen to his remonstrances. For Muthoga had completely cast a spell on her. She wanted him, longed to join the retinue of his wives and children. Indeed, since her initiation she had secretly but resolutely admired this man – his gait, his dancing, and above all his bass voice and athletic figure. Everything around him suggested mystery and power. And the courting had been short and strange. She could still remember the throbbing of her heart, his broad smile and her hesitant acceptance of a string of oyster-shells as a marriage token. This was followed by beer-drinking and the customary bride-price.

But people could not believe it and many young warriors whose offers she had brushed aside looked at her with scorn and resentment. 'Ah! Such youth and beauty to be sacrificed to an old man.' Many a one believed and in whispers declared that she was bewitched. Indeed she was: her whole heart had gone to this man.

No less memorable and sensational to her was the day they had carried her to this man's hut, a new hut that had been put up specially for her. She was going to the *shamba* when, to her surprise, three men approached her, apparently from nowhere. Then she knew. They were coming for her. She ought to have known, to have prepared herself for this. Her wedding day had come. Unceremoniously they swept her off the ground, and for a moment she was really afraid, and was putting up a real struggle to free herself from the firm yet gentle hands of the three men who were carrying her shoulder-high. And the men! the men! They completely ignored her frenzied struggles. One of them had the cheek to pinch her, 'just to keep her quiet', as he carelessly remarked to one of his companions. The pinch shocked her in a strange manner, a very pleasantly strange manner. She ceased struggling and for the first time she noticed she was riding shoulder-high on top of the soft seed-filled millet fingers which stroked her feet and sides as the men carried her. She felt really happy, but suddenly realized that she must keen all the way to her husband's home, must continue keening for a whole week.

The first season: all his love and attention lavished on her. And, in her youth, she became a target of jealousy and resentment from the other wives. A strong opposition soon grew. Oh, women. Why could they not allow her to enjoy what they had enjoyed for years – his love? She could still recall how one of them, the eldest, had been beaten for refusing to let Mukami take fire from her hut. This ended the battle of words and deeds. It was now a mute struggle. Mukami hardened towards them. She did not mind their insolence and aloofness in which they had managed to enlist the sympathy of the whole village. But why should she mind? Had not the fulfilment of her dream, ambition, life and all, been realized in this man?

Two seasons, three seasons, and the world she knew began to change. She had no child.

A *thata*! A barren woman!
No child to seal the bond between him and her!
No child to dote on, hug and scold!
No child to perpetuate the gone spirits of
Her man's ancestors and her father's blood.

She was defeated. She knew it. The others knew it too. They whispered and smiled. Oh, how their oblique smiles of insolence and pride pierced her! But she had nothing to fear. Let them be victorious. She had still got her man.

And then without warning the man began to change, and in time completely shunned her company and hut, confining himself more to his *thingira*. She felt embittered and sought him. Her heart bled for him yet found him not. Muthoga, the warrior, the farmer, the dancer, had recovered his old hardheartedness which had been temporarily subdued by her, and he began to beat her. He had found her quarrelling with the eldest wife, and all his accumulated fury, resentment and frustration seemed to find an outlet as he beat her. The beating; the crowd that watched and never helped! But that was a preamble to such torture and misery that it almost resulted in her death that very morning. He had called on her early and without warning or explanation had beaten her so much that he left her for dead. She had not screamed – she had accepted her lot. And as she lay on the ground thinking it was now the end, it dawned on her that perhaps the others had been suffering as much because of her. Yes! she could see them being beaten and crying for mercy. But she resolutely refused to let such beating and misgivings subdue her will. She must conquer; and with that she had quickly made up her mind. This was no place for her. Neither could she return to her place of birth to face her dear old considerate father again. She could not bear the shame.

The cold night breeze brought her to her present condition. Tears, long suppressed, flowed down her cheeks as she hurried down the path that wound through the bush, down the valley, through the labyrinth of thorn and bush. The murmuring stream, the quiet trees that surrounded her, did these sympathize with her or did they join with the kraal in silent denouncement of her action?

She followed the stream, and then crossed it at its lowest point where there were two or three stones on which she could step. She was still too embittered, too grieved to notice her dangerous surroundings. For was this not the place where the dead were thrown? Where the spirits of the dead hovered through the air, intermingling with the trees, molesting strangers and intruders? She was angry with the world, her husband, but more with herself. Could she have been in the wrong all the time? Was this the price she must pay for her selfish grabbing of the man's soul? But she had also sacrificed her own youth and beauty for his sake. More tears and anguish.

Oh spirits of the dead, come for me!
Oh Murungu, god of Gikuyu and Mumbi,
Who dwells on high Kerinyaga, yet is everywhere,
Why don't you release me from misery?
Dear Mother Earth, why don't you open and swallow
 me up
Even as you had swallowed Gumba – the Gumba
 who disappeared under mikongoe roots?

She invoked the spirits of the living and the dead to come and carry her off, never to be seen again.

Suddenly, as if in answer to her invocations, she heard a distant, mournful sound, pathetic yet real. The wind began to blow wildly and the last star that had so strangely comforted her vanished. She was alone in the gloom of the forest! Something cold and lifeless touched her. She jumped and at last did what the beating could not make her do – she screamed. The whole forest echoed with her scream. Naked fear now gripped her; she shook all over. And she realized that she was not alone.

Here and there she saw a thousand eyes that glowed intermittently along the stream, while she felt herself being pushed to and fro by many invisible hands. The sight and the sudden knowledge that she was in the land of ghosts, alone, and far from home, left her chilled. She could not feel, think or cry. It was fate – the will of Murungu. Lower and lower she sank onto the ground as the last traces of strength ebbed from her body. This was the end, the culmination of her dream and ambition. But it was so ironic. She did not really want to die. She only wanted a chance to start life anew – a life of giving and not only of receiving.

Her misery was not at an end, for as she lay on the ground, and even as the owl and the hyena cried in the distance, the wind blew harder, and the mournful sound grew louder and nearer; and it began to rain. The earth looked as if it would crack and open beneath her.

Then suddenly, through the lightning and thunder, she espied a tree in the distance – a huge tree it was, with the bush gently but reverently bowing all around the trunk. And she knew; she knew, that this was the tree – the sacred Mugumo – the altar of the all-seeing Murungu. 'Here at last is a place of sanctuary,' she thought.

She ran, defying the rain, the thunder and the ghosts. Her husband and the people of Muhoroini Ridge vanished into insignificance. The load that had weighed upon her heart seemed to be lifted as she ran through the thorny bush, knocking against the trees, falling and standing up. Her impotence was gone. Her worries were gone. Her one object was to reach the tree. It was a matter of life and death – a battle for life. There under the sacred Mugumo she would find sanctuary and peace. There Mukami would meet her God, Murungu, the God of her people. So she ran despite her physical weakness. And she could feel a burning inside her womb. Now she was near the place of sanctuary, the altar of the most High, the place of salvation. So towards the altar she ran, no, not running but flying; at least her soul must have been flying. For she felt as light as a feather. At last she reached the place, panting and breathless.

And the rain went on falling. But she did not hear. She had lain asleep under the protecting arms of God's tree. The spell was on her again.

Mukami woke up with a start. What! Nobody? Surely that had been Mumbi, who standing beside her husband Gikuyu had touched her – a gentle touch that went right through her body. No, she must have been dreaming. What a strange beautiful dream. And Mumbi had said, 'I am the mother of a nation.' She looked around. Darkness still. And there was the ancient tree, strong, unageing. How many secrets must you have held?

'I must go home. Go back to my husband and my people.' It was a new Mukami, humble yet full of hope, who said this. Then she fell asleep again. The spell.

The sun was rising in the east and the rich yellow-ish streaks of light filtered through the forest to where Mukami was sitting, leaning against the tree. And as the straying streaks of light touched her skin, she felt a tickling sensation that went right through her body. Blood thawed in her veins and oh! She felt warm – so very warm, happy and light. Her soul danced and her womb answered. And then she knew – knew that she was pregnant, had been pregnant for some time.

As Mukami stood up ready to go, she stared with unseeing eyes into space, while tears of deep gratitude and humility trickled down her face. Her eyes looked beyond the forest, beyond the stream, as if they were seeing something, something hidden in the distant future. And she saw the people of Muhoroini, her *airu* and her man, strong, unageing, standing amongst them. That was her rightful place, there beside her husband amongst the other wives. They must unite and support rurirī, giving it new life. Was Mumbi watching?

Far in the distance, a cow lowed. Mukami stirred from her reverie.

'I must go.' She began to move. And the Mugumo tree still stood, mute, huge and mysterious.

And The Rain Came Down!

Nyokabi dropped the big load of firewood which she had been carrying on her frail back. The load fell on the hard floor outside the door of her hut with a groaning crash. She stood for a few seconds with arms loosely akimbo, and then sat on the load, letting out a deep, enigmatic sigh. It was good to be home again. It was good and sweet to rest after a hard day's work, having laboured like a donkey.

All her life she had worked, worked, and each day brought no relief. She had thought this the best way to bury her disappointments and sorrow, but without much success. Her life seemed meaningless and as she sat there looking vacantly into space, she felt really tired, in body and spirit.

She knew she was getting old. Only a few weeks back she had looked at her reflection in a mirror only to find that her formerly rich black mass of hair was now touched with two or three ashy threads. She had shuddered and consequently swore never to look in a mirror again. So old. And no child! That was the worry. It was unthinkable. She was thata.

She had vaguely known this a long time back. The knowledge, with what it meant to her and her social standing, had given her pain in the soul. A fat worm of despair and a sense of irredeemable loss wriggled in the very marrow of her bones and was slowly eating her away.

It was a kind of hopelessness and loss of faith in human life, that comes to a person whose strong dreams and great expectations, on which he has pinned his whole life, have failed to materialize.

Nyokabi's expectations had been many. But their unvarying centre had always been 'so many' children. Ever since her initiation, she had had the one desire, to marry and have children. She always saw herself as an elderly woman with her man, sitting by a crackling fire at night, while their children, with wonder-stricken eyes and wide-open mouths, sat around listening to her yarns about her people. She had got her man, the kind of husband she had wished for, but ... but ... Murungu had not sent her anything. *He* had not answered her cry, her desire, her hope. Her great expectations had come to nought.

A biting jealousy was born in her. She avoided the company of the other women of the Ridge and also the 'healing' touch of any child. Had the women, men and children not banded together against her? Were they not all winking at one another and pointing at her? All she wanted was to shut herself in her own world.

Even the old companion of her girlhood, Njeri, who had been married and lived on the same Ridge, had suddenly become an enemy. Nyokabi's jealousy forbade her to visit Njeri or call on her whenever she gave birth, as was the general custom. Nyokabi knew nothing about Njeri's children. So you see, her fatigue was not of an hour past, but the accumulated fatigue of a lifetime. Nyokabi remembered some little lines her mother had always been fond of chanting.

> A woman without a child, a child,
> Must needs feel weary, a-weary.
> A woman without a child must lonely be,
> So God forgive her!

She sighed and looked fixedly at her mud hut where she and her man had lived for so long. It occurred to her that her mother had been singing of her. Maybe she was cursed? Maybe she was unclean? But then her man had taken her to many doctors and none had offered a real cure.

Suddenly the pain that had filled up her heart, rose and surged up her soul, up her throat. It was all real, this Thing. It was choking her; it would kill her. The nameless Thing was too much for her. She rose and began to hurry away from her hut, away from the Ridge, going she knew not whither. She was like a creature 'possessed', driven on. The fire-eye of the sun, high up in the sky, was now on its way to its own place of rest. But the woman was hurrying away from home, unable to sit or rest. The Thing would not let her.

She went up the Ridge. She felt and saw nothing. The cultivated strips of land sprawled before her, stretching down to the valley, merging with the bush and the forest. Women going home could be seen climbing up the slope carrying various loads. Njeri was amongst them. Mechanically, or as if by sheer instinct, Nyokabi avoided them. She cut across the fields and soon was in the valley. Through the bush she went, avoiding the beaten paths. The thorns tore her flesh but she pushed on, forcing her way through the labyrinth of the wild undergrowth and creeping plants. The wildness of the place, and the whole desolate atmosphere seemed to have strangely harmonized with her state of madness. Even now, she did not know where she was going. Soon she found herself in a part of the forest where she had never been before. No light shone through and the heavens seemed to have changed. She could not see the smiling clouds any more, for the forest was very dense. For the first time, she hesitated, fearing to plunge deeper into the mysteries of the forest. But this nameless Thing urged her on, on.

A long rock stood in the forest. It looked inviting to a weary traveller. Nyokabi sat on it. She was beginning to come to her senses but she was still very confused and physically worn out. She could hardly tell the time or how long she had been walking. A voice spoke to her, not loudly, but in whispers –

'... Woman, if you stay here, you'll die – the haunted death of a lonely woman.'

She did not want to die. Not just yet. She stood up and dragged herself up. The heavy cloud of forlorn despair still weighed on her. But at last she managed to pull herself into the open. Open? No. The whole country looked dull. The sun seemed to have died prematurely and a dull greyness had blanketed the earth. A cold wind began to blow and carried rubbish whirling up in the air. The heavens wore a wrinkled face and little angry clouds were gathering. Then flash, flash and a deafening crash! The heavens shook and the earth trembled beneath her feet. And without further warning the rain came down.

At first she was too amazed, too overpowered to move. A tickling sensation went right through her as the first few drops of rain touched her skin. Yes! The first delicate drops of rain had a soothing effect and she felt as if she could open her cold heart to the cold rain. She wanted to cry or shout 'Come! Come rain! Wash me, drench me to cold death!'

As if the rain had heard her dumb cry, it poured

down with great vigour. Its delicate touch was gone. It was now beating her with a growing fury. This was frightening. She had to hurry home if she was not going to be drenched to death. She was now running frantically with all the vigour she could muster. She gasped with fear and all her life seemed to have become concentrated into one struggle – the struggle to extricate herself from the cold fury of the rain. But she could not keep up the struggle. The rain was too strong for a weary woman. So, when she approached the top, she decided to walk and abandon herself to the rain.

And then she heard the delicate but passionate cry of a human voice. Her womanly instinct told her it was a child's cry. She stopped and looked to the left. The rain had ebbed a little and so the cry could be heard clearly, coming from a small clustered bush just down the slope. The idea of going down again when her goal was so near was sheer agony for Nyokabi. This was a moment of trial; the moment rarely given to us to prove our worth as human beings. The moment is rare. It comes and if not taken goes by, leaving us forever regretful.

Virtually worn out, her goal under her very nose, the old jealousy came and gnawed at her even more sharply. To save another's child! She began to climb up … up … But the rain came down again with renewed vigour, and a howl, at once passionate and frightened, rose above the fury of the rain. Nyokabi's heart almost stopped. She could not take another step. For the cry remained ringing in her heart. She turned round and began to go down the Ridge to the little bush, though she was tired and knew not whether she would be able to climb up again. The child, about two or three years old, lay huddled in a small shelter that had, until a few moments before, protected him from the rain.

Nyokabi did not ask anything but took the child in her arms. She tried to protect the child with her body as she began to climb up again, barely able to lift her legs. But, oh, the warmth! The sweet revitalizing warmth that flows from one stream of life into another! Nyokabi's blood thawed and danced in her veins. She gained renewed hope and faith as she went up, treading dangerously over the slippery ground. She cried, 'Let me save him. Give me time, oh Murungu, to save him. Then let me die!' The rain seemed not to heed her prayer or to pity her because of her additional weight. She had to fight it out alone. But her renewed faith in living gave her strength and she was nearing the top when she slipped off the ground and fell. She woke up, undaunted, ready for the struggle. What did it matter if the child was not hers? Had the child not given her warmth, a warmth that rekindled her cold heart? So she fought on, the child clinging to her for protection.

Literally dragging her legs along, she reached the top. Then the rain stopped.

Wholly drenched, weary and hungry, Nyokabi trudged quietly across the Ridge towards her hut. Victory surged in her blood. A new light shone in her eyes, as if challenging the coming dusk. Her victory had overcome her very real physical exhaustion. She reached her hut, fell on the bed.

Her man was frantic with fright and worry. Nyokabi did not seem to see him. She only pointed at the child, and he wrapped him in dry clothes. He also brought some for his wife and added more wood to the bright fire, all the time wondering where Nyokabi had got the child.

Nyokabi had fallen into a sort of delirium and she was muttering '... Rain ... Rain ... came ... down ...' Then she would lose herself in some inaudible words.

After a time, he took a better look at the child. Nyokabi had by now fallen asleep and so could not see the look of surprise in her husband's face as he recognized the child as being no other than Njeri's youngest. At first he could not understand, and wondered how his 'jealous' wife could have come into contact with the child.

Then he remembered. He had met Njeri running frantically all over the Ridge looking for her child, who she said had eluded the other children. Great pride surged in Nyokabi's man as he went out with the sleeping child to break the news. To think his wife had done *this*!

At long last, I also came to believe that she was mad. It was natural. For my mother said that she was mad. And everybody in the village seemed to be of the same opinion. Not that the old woman ever did anything really eccentric as mad people do. She never talked much. But sometimes she would fall a victim to uncontrollable paroxysms of laughter for no apparent reason. Perhaps they said so because she stared at people hard as if she was seeing something beyond them. She had sharp glittering eyes whose 'liveness' stood in deep contrast to her wrinkled, emaciated body. But there was something in that woman's eyes that somehow suggested mystery and knowledge, and right from the beginning shook my belief in her madness. What was the something and where was it? It may have been in her, or in the way she looked at people, or simply in the way she postured and carried herself. It may have been in any one of these, or in all of them at once.

I had occasion to mention this woman and my observations about her to my father. He just looked at me and then quietly said, 'Perhaps it is sorrow. This burning sun, this merciless drought ... running into our heads making us turn white and mad!'

I didn't then know why he said this. I still believe that he was not answering my question but rather was speaking his thoughts aloud. But he was right – I mean, right about 'whiteness'.

For the whole country appeared white – the whiteness of death.

From ridge up to ridge the neat little shambas stood bare. The once short and beautiful hedges – the product of land consolidation and the pride of farmers in our district – were dry and powdered with dust. Even the old mugumo tree that stood just below our village, and which was never dry, lost its leaves and its greenness – the living greenness that had always scorned short-lived droughts. Many people had forecast doom. Weather-prophets and medicine-men – for some still remain in our village though with diminished power – were consulted by a few people and all forecast doom.

Radio boomed. And 'the weather forecast for the next twenty-four hours', formerly an item of news of interest only to would-be travellers, became news of first importance to everyone. Yes. Perhaps those people at K.B.S.* and the Met. Department were watching, using

_____
* Kenya Broadcasting Service

150

their magic instruments for telling weather. But men and women in our village watched the clouds with their eyes and waited. Every day I saw my father's four wives and other women in the village go to the shamba. They just sat and talked, but actually they were waiting for the great hour when God would bring rain. Little children who used to play in the streets, the dusty streets of our new village, had stopped and all waited, watching, hoping.

Many people went hungry. We were lucky in our home – unlike most families – because one of my brothers worked in Nairobi and another at Limuru.

That remark by my father set me thinking more seriously about the old woman. At the end of the month, when my mother bought some yams and njahi beans at the market, I stole some and in the evening went about looking for the mud hut that belonged to the woman. I found it. It was in the very heart of the village. That was my first meeting with the woman. I have gone there many times. Yet that evening still remains the most vivid of all. I found her huddled in a dark corner while the dying embers of a few pieces of wood in the fireplace flickered slightly, setting grotesque shadows over the mud walls. I was frightened and wanted to run away. I did not. I called her 'grandmother' – though I don't think she was really so old as to warrant that – and gave her the yams. She looked at them and then at me. Her eyes brightened a little. Then she lowered her face and began wailing.

'I thought it was "him" come back to me,' she sobbingly said. And then: 'Oh, the drought has ruined me!'

I could not bear the sight and ran away quickly, wondering if my father had known it all. Perhaps she was mad.

A week later, she told me about 'him'. Words cannot recreate the sombre atmosphere in that darkish hut as she incoherently told me all about her life-long struggle with droughts.

As I have said, we had all, for months on end, sat and watched, waiting for the rain. The night before the day when the first few drops of rain fell was marked with an unusual solitude and weariness infecting everybody. There was no noise in the streets. The woman, watching by the side of her only son, heard nothing. She just sat on a three-legged Gikuyu stool and watched the dark face of the boy as he wriggled in agony on the narrow bed near the fireplace. When the dying fire occasionally flickered, it revealed a dark face now turned white. Ghostly shadows flitted across the walls as if mocking the lone watcher by the bedside. And the boy kept on asking, 'Do you think I'll die, Mother?' She did not know what to say or do. She could only hope and pray. And yet the pleading voice of the hungry boy kept on insisting, 'Mother, I don't want to die.' But the mother looked on helplessly. She felt as if her strength and will had left her. And again the accusing voice: 'Mother, give me something to eat.' Of course he did not know, could not know, that the woman had nothing, had finished her last ounce of flour. She had already decided not to trouble her neighbours again for they had sustained her for more than two months. Perhaps they had also drained their resources. Yet the boy kept on looking reproachingly at her as if he would accuse her of being without mercy.

What could a woman without her man do? She had lost him during the Emergency, killed not by Mau Mau or the Colonial forces, but poisoned at a beer-drinking party. At least that is what people said, just because it had been such a sudden death. He was not there now to help her watch over the boy. To her this night in 1961 was so different from such another night in the '40s when two of her sons died one after the other because of drought and hunger. That was during the 'Famine of Cassava' as it was called because people ate flour made from cassava. Then her man had been with her to bear part of the grief. Now she was alone. It seemed so unfair to her. Was it a curse in the family? She thought so, for she herself would never have been born but for the lucky fact that her mother had been saved from such another famine by missionaries. That was just before the real advent of the white men. Ruraya Famine (the Famine of England) was the most serious famine to have ever faced the Gikuyu people. Her grandmother and grandfather had died and only she, from their family, had been saved. Yes. All the menace of droughts came to her as she watched the accusing, pleading face of the boy. Why was it only her? Why not other women? This her only child, got very late in life.

She left the hut and went to the headman of the village. Apparently he had nothing. And he seemed not to understand her. Or to understand that droughts could actually kill. He thought her son was suffering from his old illnesses which had always attacked him. Of course she had thought of this too. Her son had always been an ailing child. But she had never taken him to the hospital. Even now she would not. No, no, not even the hospital would take him from her. She preferred doing everything for him, straining herself for the invalid. And this time she knew it was hunger that was killing him. The headman told her that the D.O. these days rationed out food – part of the Famine Relief Scheme in the drought-stricken areas. Why had she not heard of this earlier? That night she slept, but not too well for the invalid kept on asking, 'Shall I be well?'

The queue at the D.O.'s place was long. She took her ration and began trudging home with a heavy heart. She did not enter but sat outside, strength ebbing from her knees. And women and men with strange faces streamed from her hut without speaking to her. But there was no need. She knew that her son was gone and would not return.

The old woman never once looked at me as she told me all this. Now she looked up and continued, 'I am an old woman now. The sun has set on my only child; the drought has taken him. It is the will of God.' She looked down again and poked the dying fire.

I rose to go. She had told me the story brokenly yet in words that certainly belonged to no mad woman. And that night (it was Sunday or Saturday) I went home wondering why some people were born to suffer and endure so much misery.

I last talked to the old woman about two or three weeks ago. I cannot remember well as I have a bad memory. Now it has rained. In fact it has been raining for about a week, though just thin showers. Women are busy planting. Hope for all is mounting.

Real torrential rain began yesterday. It set in early. Such rain had not been witnessed for years. I went to the old woman's hut with a gift, this time not of yams and beans, but of sweet potatoes. I opened the door and found her huddled up in her usual corner. The fire was out. Only a flickering yellow flame of a lighted lantern lingered on. I spoke to her. She slightly raised her head. In the waning cold light, she looked white. She opened her eyes a little. Their usual unearthly brightness was intensified a thousand times. Only there was something else in them. Not sadness. But a hovering spot of joy, or exultation, as if she had found something long-lost, long-sought. She tried to smile, but there was something unearthly, something almost diabolical and ugly in it. She let out words, weakly, speaking not directly to me, but actually declaring aloud her satisfaction, or relief.

'I see them all now. All of them waiting for me at the gate. And I am going . . .'

Then she bent down again. Almost at once the struggling lantern light went out, but not before I had seen in a corner all my gifts; the food had never been touched but had been stored there. I went out.

The rain had stopped. Along the streets, through the open doors, I could see lighted fires flickering, and hear people chattering and laughing.

At home we were all present. My father was there. My mother had already finished cooking. My brothers and sisters chattered on, about the rain and the drought that was now over. My father was quiet and thoughtful as usual. I also was quiet. I did not join in the talk, for my mind was still on the 'mad' woman and my untouched gifts of food. I was just wondering if she too had gone with the drought and hunger. Just then, one of my brothers mentioned the woman and made a jocular remark about her madness. I stood up and glared at him.

'Mad indeed!' I almost screamed. And everybody stared at me in startled fear. All of them, that is, except my father, who kept on looking at the same place.

Winning

by Casey Plett

He's shivering, Zoe thought as she came in Robin's bedroom and saw his tall muscle-and-pudge body vibrating on the bed, blanket on the floor. She made to tuck the blanket back over him when she saw his face was contorted and his lips were moving like waves.

She said hey and softly rocked his shoulder. Robin gasped then his face turned instantly blithe.

Hey, sorry to wake you.

'S okay, he said. He stretched and his boxers made a ruffling noise on the sheets. You leaving? he said.

Yes, she said. Thanks for letting me crash.

Definitely. Boy, he yawned, I feel fucked up. Robin'd finished most of a magnum last night. Zoe'd had two glasses then switched to milk. She loved milk.

She giggled and said awww and mussed his wavy brown hair. It was silly, she realized, walking outside and zipping her hoodie up over her dress, but she had forgotten that boys even had nightmares.

It was mid-November, when in the Pacific North-west the panorama of clouds stopped flirting with the sky and moved in and set parking brakes until May. A soft mist patter of rain was coming down as Zoe walked down the motel-like stairs of Robin's complex, then over to Eugene Station to take the 66 north. She got on and texted her best friend Julia, back in New York: *Hi. You're beautiful and I miss you to fucking pieces.* When she got off the bus and walked up to Ayers the rain had stopped but the sky was still an ocean of pearl grey. Zoe hated this. *Humans aren't supposed to go months with all their sunlight broken,* she thought. She had actually loved the winters in New York. Everyone there complained about grey but to Zoe, New York had been sunny and bright.

Back at her mom's, the boxes in the kitchen hadn't moved. There was a note on the counter. *Gone to Farmer's Market one last time. I need everything out of your room TONIGHT.*

Well, that was a new request. She still had a week to stay here, but whatever.

She went into her room and resumed clearing out her shit. *You can build up so much stuff when you have a room in a house you don't actually live in,* she thought. And Zoe'd always been a pack rat. Especially as a teenager. She would save a lot of things she thought regular families saved for their kids. She'd dumped most of that stuff now though, and there were only a few boxes left, orderly seas of social studies papers, choir programs, stuff like that.

Sandy came home as Zoe was mashing a basketball-sized paper wad into the recycling.

I bought some fruit for you, Sandy said.

I'm not hungry, said Zoe.

Don't give me that. Have you eaten?

I don't want any fruit, thanks.

Sandy washed a bag of Bartlett pears and plunked it dripping on the counter. She put her elbows beside the bag and massaged her eyes. Better to tell me the truth, don't you think? she said.

Ever since Zoe transitioned, Sandy had become convinced that her daughter would develop an eating disorder, though Zoe was eating as little as ever.

No thanks Mom, Zoe said. I'm not hungry.

Zoe? Sandy said. The last thing I want to do is have to make you eat. It's not like I like having this conversation.

Sandy was trans too. Zoe had come out to her exactly eighteen months ago, on the phone, from her Brooklyn apartment, after she'd already been on hormones for a while. She'd meticulously taken steps to avoid telling her, and when she had her mother had cried and cried.

Her phone pulsed and Zoe saw the text from Julia: *You're beautiful. I miss you.* Zoe picked up the biggest pear and took a gargantuan bite. What do you need help with next? she asked.

*

Sandy had done a lot to have Zoe with Sandy's wife at the time, Taya. This was back in the mid-eighties. Sandy'd sent a forged death certificate to the clinic where she'd banked her sperm, who then sent the samples to a friend of Taya's, a nurse practitioner, who then helped with inseminating. This was on the plains, where Sandy and Taya had grown up. They'd moved to Oregon to have Zoe, who was born downtown in an apartment off 8th. Zoe loved this story, and she never got tired of telling it to her friends back East. She liked to say she had been born loved. Though Taya'd left both of them when Zoe was eight, and Sandy hadn't always been the most stable of mothers, Zoe had always felt acres of love.

Can you go through the closet in the spare room? Sandy said.

No problem, said Zoe.

Hey, have another pear if you want it, they're completely yours! Sandy called after her. Zoe didn't respond so she got out pita bread and hummus and went to her desk in the living room to do paperwork.

She passed well, her mother did. Zoe had always admired her for that, and she especially admired it now. In the old days no one had known about Sandy, and with her being six-one and broad-shouldered and poor, Zoe thought, it really couldn't have been easy. I always wore jeans, Sandy told Zoe once, when Zoe was seventeen. It had been the fifth anniversary of Sandy's bottom surgery and she'd been unusually talkative. I always wore jeans, she said, almost never skirts or dresses. Because just in people's heads, subconsciously, the idea of trannies wearing jeans doesn't mesh. Zoe had listened to this raptly. They said I looked mannish, Sandy giggled, but they never thought I was a man! I tricked 'em. She sounded like she was gloating. She said, they just passed me off as some big earthy dyke. Well you know, that's okay.

From very early in her childhood, Zoe knew that Sandy had once lived as a man. Neither mom had hidden it from her, but it was also understood to be a buried subject, something gravely serious Zoe wasn't supposed to talk or ask about.

I did have some really pretty dresses, Sandy had said in that conversation. But I had to be very careful about wearing them. I just had to be careful.

They'd moved out of the apartment off 8th when Zoe was in third grade. It had been right after Taya left, and right when Sandy got her job with the county. That's when they got one of the few bungalows left along Ayers, on the north edge of town just shy of the city line. Sandy was from the country, and she missed the stars, she said. She missed the stars, and the quiet.

*

Robin called a couple hours later, as Zoe was muscling a box down from the top of the closet. Hey! he said. Do you want a job?

Um, Zoe said. Huh. Um. Fuck. I don't know. I want to go back to Brooklyn but I do need money and—Then suddenly she sneezed, inflecting her expulsion up at the end like a squeak: *AAAACHoo!*

Jesus dude! Bless you, said Robin.

Um, thanks.

So what was that? You're going back to Brooklyn? Well hey, that's great, he said. I'm happy for you.

Zoe lowered her head and leaned against the wall. It made a *thunk*. No, she said to Robin, never mind. Yes. Yes I need a job. I would love a job. What's the job.

Oh! You're staying! he exploded. I love it! I love you! You will love it back here! You will love me! You will love everything! You will re-fall in love with the Northwest! I promise!

Zoe giggled a little. What's the job, dammit.

It's doing phone surveys for the government? Robin said, hesitant.

You're fucking kidding, she said before she could stop herself. Then she said shit, I'm sorry, you're being nice here. Tell me more.

It's eleven an hour, Robin said. It's not that bad! I did it when I moved back and it was a good way to get on my feet. It might be the same for you, he said. He stopped talking. Zoe stayed with her head against the wall not speaking.

Just thought I'd offer, Robin said. You wanna come out tonight? I could tell you more about it.

Sure, let's talk tonight.

Cool. Also you're going to have to have more than one drink.

No I don't!

The rain patter was stronger and steady outside, the periodic thrum of these months that sometimes made Zoe think of a long, unbroken rustle of leaves. She showered, shaved, changed into a crinkly black polka-dotted dress and sweater tights, put on makeup and went to say goodbye to her mom.

You still wear tights this time of year? Sandy said.

Yup.

That for the boys?

Oh Jesus Christ, Mom.

It's just a question, Sandy said. Hey I forgot to tell you. I'm not leaving on the first anymore. Staying here 'til the tenth. Soooo you'll need to stay here longer.

Zoe nodded and said, I think I can make that work. Yes, that should be fine. She said it enunciated and slowly, as if she actually had to consider her answer. Or as if she hadn't a month ago jettisoned her life and rent-indebted roommates back in Brooklyn to return to Oregon for the first time in years. It had been Sandy's suggestion: Zoe'd been talking about how broke she was and Sandy'd been like hey well look. Why don't you come back here for a bit. Get on your feet a little. I need help moving out anyway and I don't know what to do with all your stuff. It wasn't the first time Sandy'd asked her to move back home (I'd rather grow a second dick, Zoe'd once said, calm and icy, when Sandy wouldn't leave it alone), but she'd lost her job in summer and her debt was piling up and she'd crashed on a few couches but eventually she just didn't have a lot of options. And whatever, she'd thought, it'd be temporary anyway, she was a grown-up, she could stand living with her mom for a month or two and she could always leave if she had to. Maybe it'd even be good for them, Zoe had thought. Maybe it'd be peaceful, like they'd re-learn some good parent-kid relationship things.

And to her surprise, so far, they generally had.

Now Sandy said cool, cool. Know what you're doing yet when I'm out of here?

Zoe shook her head.

Sandy sighed then caught herself and waved. Ah, she said, you'll figure it out.

Her mother was eating chips and salsa and spilling occasionally, thick blood-dot trails between her and the bowl. Zoe realized that she smelled pot.

Zoe'd hated weed as a kid. It did calm her mother,

but it also made her forgetful and dumb. She'd flake on getting Zoe from school, leave the house without telling her, stuff like that. It used to scare Zoe, and then around high school it just made her angry. She'd made her peace with the stuff as an adult though.

It had cold-snapped today and Zoe put on her coat. I'll see you tomorrow? she said.

Sure sure sure, Sandy said. Just be safe, okay? I want you to remember to be safe.

I will, yes, I promise, Mom, Zoe said. She turned around and put on her gloves and hat and bugged her eyes once she was out the door. Waiting for the 66, she saw a younger girl in only a hoodie and scarf, shivering with her hood up. *It's like no one wants to dress warm here*, Zoe thought. As if because it almost never got *cold*-cold, people didn't want to turn on heat, put on coats, cover extremities. So they were colder here than they were in places that were actually cold.

Walking to the bar from the bus station, a girl younger than Zoe and wearing clothes that had all turned the same color asked for a quarter and Zoe pulled a fingerful of change from her wallet. The girl mumbled a thank you and Zoe saluted with her fingers and said yeah lady.

It's gay night! Robin said when Zoe sat down at a table.

Eugene has a gay night now?

Yeah, that's what I thought too when I got back. But hey, there are drag queens, you'll like that.

Zoe looked around. Most of the twenty-odd people in the bar looked like Robin, young and punk-hipster-ish and straight.

Wait, shit, should I not say that? he said. Are drag queens bad?

No, Zoe shook her head, no. Drag queens are great.

I can't tell if you're being serious or not.

Can we talk about something else?

Sure, sure, sorry, said Robin. They were silent then he said get a drink goddammit!

The bartender was a guy Zoe'd gone to high school with. Zoe hadn't seen him since they'd graduated. She figured he knew about her transitioning. Thanks to Facebook, everyone knew about her transitioning.

HEY! said Zoe.

WOAH! HEY! said the bartender. ZOE! She liked that. Just *Zoe.* None of this *Zoe? So . . . it's Zoe, right?* Or her old name then *Sorry! It's just weird to think of you as a Zoe!* Robin had said that so earnestly and emotionally once and it had made her cry.

But the bartender. He was better-looking than Zoe remembered: Tall, with curly black hair, a slight beer belly. He was wearing a Huey Lewis & the News T-shirt. His name was—

Fuck why couldn't she fucking remember his fucking name?

Get a rum and diet? she asked.

He mixed her drink and stuck a purple umbrella in the glass. She ran through memories of people they'd had in common. There was Frankie—

Oh holy fuck. A lightning bolt of memory went through her. *Frankie.* Frankie Pringle was a girl Zoe'd been close with but drifted apart from after high school. Well hey, here's a weird question for you, Zoe said.

What?

You still see Frankie at all?

Frankie Pringle?

Yeah.

No. Not for years. We fell out of touch, there was just, y'know, some bad shit.

Zoe nodded like she was trying to be thoughtful. Yeah. Bad shit.

I know she's back in town though, he said. Last I heard she was getting in deep with the nose candy.

Really? Zoe said. She'd known her share of coke-heads back in New York but she'd never have guessed Frankie—

Okay, Zoe said, thanks anyway. Just curious.

The music got louder. You like the umbrella? he hollered and smiled huge.

Zoe giggled. Yeah! she said. It's flashy! Thanks!

She did a small wave and said good seeing you, then went back to the table.

So apparently, Robin said suddenly, some like, student-bro types have been shooting homeless people lately.

Zoe opened her mouth and swizzled her drink. What? No, she said. Jesus Christ.

It's weird, dude, he said. It's weird. Like, they used BBs, not bullets. But still. You'd think it's such a quiet little town, you know?

You'd think, Zoe said. She looked at Robin's face, open-mouthed, almost awe-struck, and she turned sour. She took a long drink. So what's this job about, she said.

Robin gulped his beer. Okay. So it's like, you come in, they tell you what survey you're doing that day, you read a little sheet about it, and then you call the numbers on your list. And some people do 'em and some don't. It's not hard. They pay you eleven an hour no matter what.

That's good. How many hours? On average? she asked.

Twenty-five.

Not bad.

You'd have the job, Robin insisted. I know it. My boss loved me, like, he *really* liked me. I guess who's to say but I'm pretty sure I was one of the best people there. If I called him tomorrow and told him how awesome you were? He would probably hire you.

Thanks . . . Zoe drifted off. I don't know. I do need money, I just don't know if I want to—

Oh for chrissakes, she thought. Even if she was sure about going back to New York there was no way she was getting there soon, and talking on the phone was as appealing as shoveling shit but whatever, there were worse jobs out there.

You know what, she said. Sounds great. Thanks. Sign me up.

Cool! Okay. Hey, how're you doing back here anyway? Robin had the serious, concerned look on his face that sometimes drove Zoe up the goddamn wall.

You always ask me that, honey! Zoe said. I'm fine.

Robin and Zoe had known each other since they were little, but they'd gotten tight in high school because of theater. They'd both been drawn into tech, she lights and he sound, and they ended up board op-ing something like six shows together. They'd been kind of a duo, actually. They were known for a lot of wiseass shit. Once during a full tech run for the spring musical they'd interrupted a climactic scene in a church by overlaying death metal and a wash of blood red.

Robin'd been a gas-station-jacket kind of emo kid back then so a lot of people thought he was into dudes, to which he'd say no, Zoe was the one guy he'd ever go gay for, and to which Zoe would say stuff like that's sweet but I hope your dick grows bigger. Most people didn't question it. They were those boys. They weren't besties, they just had their thing. They'd given each other flowers at graduation. And Robin'd always stayed in touch, in his own way, posted dumb videos on her wall, sent a little *Woah, congrats girl!* message when she transitioned. Zoe'd always liked that he did those things, and she liked how the two of them hung. She liked how their friendship could be close without being intimate.

Hey, see that bartender? Zoe said.

Robin shifted in his seat. You mean Al?

Al! That's his fucking name! she said. I've been trying to remember.

Robin snickered. You forgot about Al?

He's cuter than I remember, said Zoe. Robin laughed awkwardly and said hah, that's funny. She took another drink. *Hey!* she said. Shit. I can't believe I haven't asked you this yet. Do you know what Frankie's up to?

HOLY SHIT! Robin pounded a fist on the table. He wasn't even drunk, he could just get that excited. I never told you about her! Fuck man. Okay. You know we lived together?

Zoe shook her head and he said well we did. It was my last place in Portland before I came back here last year. But I didn't get all my stuff out right away so I went back a few months after to get it, and dude, Frankie was pregnant.

Zoe's mouth unhinged slightly. Yeah, Robin said. Like six or seven months along. That was this February, so she must've had the kid by now. Zoe blew a tuft of black hair out of her face. It was weird, Robin said, to see her that big, you know? Zoe nodded; Frankie had always been sickly-skinny. Apparently, Robin continued, she gave it to some super Portland-y gay dude couple in Sellwood? That's the rumor anyway. Who knows.

What do you mean the rumor? You didn't talk about it?

No, said Robin. I tried. I said are you keeping it? She said no and I was like hey I know we're not really friends anymore but do you want to talk about it? And she just lit a cigarette—in her own fucking apartment too—and went into her room. And then her boyfriend or whoever he was, some dude—not to be mean, but you know how Frankie's always had some dude—this dude just sitting there, he squinted at me like *I* was some sort of asshole, so I got my stuff and left.

Oh.

Robin frowned and rubbed the side of his face. Yeah, no one's heard anything solid about her since. Like I said, there's rumors, but I don't know for sure. Sometimes

I wish I'd done more, I dunno, but shit. She just fucked up, like, a *lot*, and not just with our rent, you heard about her dad, right?

Her phone buzzed. It was a text from Sandy. *Your room is a shithole. I love you!* She scooped the phone from the table and dropped it in her bag.

I know he's gone, said Zoe.

Frankie's dad had been great, a kind and gentle older man. He'd gotten cancer and died a few years ago. It had been sudden and sad. She'd left a message on Frankie's voicemail but couldn't fly out for the funeral.

Robin shook his head and said she abandoned him. She wouldn't leave Portland to see him. She had all these excuses, like, about work or how her uncle was looking after him, but she almost never went down. She saw him like three or four times. It was fucked up.

What?! He was like the best dad ever! That is really weird! Zoe said.

Yeah. I just didn't get it, I guess.

Zoe had sometimes wondered what Frankie would think of her now. She wondered if Frankie would have wanted to hang out with her, if she would talk to her the same way, if she would—Zoe hated admitting this to herself, but—if Frankie would still think she was pretty.

Frankie'd been this tall girl, roughly Zoe's size, with small tits and bright blue chest-length hair. Zoe'd go over to her place on Willakenzie and Frankie'd loan her clothes and teach her things like how to cover her beard shadow, line her eyes so it was just barely noticeable. And how to flat-iron her hair and deep-color coordinate and all that shit.

She was the only one Zoe ever did that with in high school; she'd never said anything about wanting to be a girl either, and Frankie never asked. It just kind of happened one day. They were hanging out in her room and Frankie said okay sorry if this sounds weird but I was just thinking you would look *really* good in this one thing I have. And it went from there and it was like they both knew better than to talk too deeply about it. Zoe'd never told anybody about this stuff, not even later in New York. It had been so surreal at the time that it never took up the front burner space of her memory. Only a few times a year, even after transitioning, would she remember snatches of being in Frankie's room. It always startled her. How easily she could forget it happened at all.

And Frankie once had looked at Zoe and cupped her chin and said God, you're beautiful. She was never exasperated with Zoe's tics or—as a lot of cis women would later be to Zoe—bitter or nasty or bitchy or jealous or any flavor of mean at all, really. She'd only taken care of Zoe, sisterly and lovingly. But then Zoe'd gone to New York and Frankie'd gone to Portland, and they tried to keep up with the odd text and call and stuff, but they were never back home at the same time and Frankie hated Facebook and pretty quickly their contact just petered out.

Zoe returned a text to Julia then said to her mom *Sorry, I'll fix it, I love you too.* People finally started to fill the bar, wet with rain and their hair stringy. Zoe remarked on this to Robin.

It's probably because the Ducks just finished playing, he said. Zoe let out a hoot. Dude, she said. Only in Eugene are all the gays at the football game.

The supervisor at the survey place interviewed Zoe for ten minutes and told her to show up the next day at four.

The following afternoon, Zoe put on a white button-up blouse and a purple pencil skirt and got there early. Hey hey new girl! said the supervisor. He seated Zoe at a desk with a stack of green hard-backed paper and a list of numbers and a phone. She made her first dial and drew a long line on a piece of scratch paper. A cheerful man from Elgin answered and she talked to him about his hay cuttings. She had drawn a lot more lines on the scratch paper by the time he hung up. She made a second phone call and the man swore about Obama so intensely Zoe got flustered in her questions, and then the guy yelled now wait a minute, am I talking to a boy or a girl? A girl, sir, Zoe said weakly. He hung up a lot sooner. She pressed a hand to her cheek and looked around; everybody else was busy calling.

On her third call, she stuttered a bit because the man on the phone, a surly dairy farmer outside Pacific City, sounded exactly like a man she'd known back in New York, a guy with layered blond hair who ran a bar in Williamsburg wallpapered with covers of Gaddis books. They had gone out for dinner, then out dancing. He'd been amazingly charming, gentlemanly. She'd accepted all the drinks he bought her and back at his place he'd begun squeezing her nipples and slipping his hands south and her last memory was of mushily shaking her head wait, hold on, I like you, I want to, just like, wait. And when she woke up she was on his bed, alone, and he was at his desk on his computer, and both sides of her bottom had a dull, vomit-spurning ache.

How many milk-giving cows did you say? said Zoe. I'm sorry? Including heifers that are not ye—

Fifty. Two, said the man. Now do you have it this time or do I need to repeat it again! You tell me here! and Zoe said yes, of course, of course sir, and by nine o'clock Zoe had covered the scratch paper with black-and-white penciled swirls and shapes, crisscrossing paisleys and hectograms and triple helixes and the outlines of faces.

Some of the faces resembled her mom.

Her mom.

Zoe had always seen Sandy as dimly gorgeous. She had short coiffed ash-blonde hair like Sharon Stone in *Casino* without the rattails, wore blue or grey skinny jeans, tank tops with shiny satin edges that showed off lightly-muscled swimmer's arms, and long earrings that skittered around her collarbone whenever she moved her head. In winter she wore cable-knit zippered hoodies. Zoe, on the other hand, kept her hair black, liked dresses with stripes or polka-dots, see-through blouses over camisoles, patterned sweater tights in winter. She sped through tubes of eyeliner and lipstick, Sandy maybe used a little mascara once in a while. Even as Zoe took no part of her own style from her—if she had to be honest, she dressed a bit like her other mother Taya, who now spoiled her with clothes on visits—Zoe did admire the way Sandy looked.

She admired a lot about her mother, really.

She admired the way she hadn't hid from Zoe the pain of Taya leaving her, but she rarely bad-mouthed or castigated Taya herself.

(And given that Taya had departed with a load of their money and a note including the words "Like anyone else would have loved you," she would've had plenty of reason.)

She admired how Sandy'd treated Zoe's boyfriends in high school, the ones she dragged up from South or the U of O (no gay boys were out at her own school) and how Sandy welcomed them and cooked for them even when sometimes they were snotty to her.

She admired the sex talk Sandy had given her when she was really young, before puberty. Sandy had told her: *Now, this is a thing teenagers and adults like to do and they get to do. Kids don't, it's not a kid thing, you won't even want to do it and you shouldn't. But this is what'll happen when you're older. And it can be wonderful. But it's important you're safe. There's a safe way to do it and an unsafe way, it's like driving without a seatbelt, where if something bad happens you can die but if you're safe it gives you freedom, you can't imagine, the happiness and the freedom. When you're older, I will help you and we can talk about it. This is something I want you to do right and it's something I want you to look forward to. I want this to be a good and healthy part of your life.* Zoe really admired that, especially when she found out about all of Sandy's friends who'd died during what she'd only refer to as the plague. Zoe had remembered a few of them, from when she was a kid. But only faintly, and only a few.

Thanks for your time sir, Zoe said to her last call.

Yeah, yeah, good night ma'am, the man grumbled. Zoe folded the drawings she made, thought of sticking them in her bag, then dropped them in the trash, not the recycling, the trash.

So New York huh?! the supervisor asked as they left the building together. Why'd you come here?

Zoe was tired of answering that question and lately she'd just been snapping *I'm helping my mom!* in a tone that made everyone think her mom had a deadly illness and needed Zoe to tend to her last days. Or something. It usually got people to leave her alone. But when she said that now her supervisor just said huh. Do you like it here though, like do you think you want to stay here?

Zoe considered how to answer that to a stranger.

Well, I grew up here, she said softly.

Walking down darkened slick Willamette Street with her hoodie up in the sprinkle-mist rain, it occurred to her that she'd walked these streets late often since coming back but hadn't been propositioned or harassed once in Eugene. Or been made to feel unsafe in any way, really.

When Zoe was a kid she thought she lived in a great town, she thought no place was better than this little city (a term Taya had liked to use, *oh, this little city.*) Zoe didn't like the neighborhood they'd ended up in, a weird little bumpkin-and-religious-yuppie enclave, but she loved downtown and she loved the U of O and she even loved the dumb political battles that played out in the city: Bike paths through the Catholic school, the cross on Skinner's Butte, where to build the new hospital; all the little clashes between right and left, hippies and Mormons, developers and enviros. It had felt like that stupid idea of what America was supposed to be. And no one was from there. It was a place you moved to. Even from middle school on, it seemed like being born in town put her in the minority. When she was a teenager, leaving just didn't occur to her, like, why would you do that if you were lucky enough to be *from* here? She thought when she left home she'd just get a room in a house back downtown by the WOW Hall and go be a stupid Duck for four years, then get a job and a little house of her own then there she be, there she be! as her mom would say, in one of her few kept Midwesternisms. Zoe was rarely bitter about being trans; if you needed to believe in the possibility of unbitter trans women, Zoe'd be your girl. But she knew she wouldn't have left if it hadn't been for that. She would've stayed, gone to the Country Fair, signed on with a co-op, checked in on her mom, lived the Beautiful New Liberal American life. It had been so close. Hell, on the face of it, the town in its current era had been designed specifically for someone like her, like, who else if not for the fag kid of a woman like Sandy, queer and transplanted and a hippie to boot. Zoe had really always thought it was a great town. She'd never hated it growing up, ever, ever, ever. But she knew staying meant a boy future, a pretend-to-be-cis future; she didn't have the strength to figure out the gender thing around everyone she'd known. She knew that in part from her mom. You couldn't transition and keep everything else in your life the same. Couldn't happen. She tested it a bit one summer by telling a few friends about Sandy, the ones she thought would react the best and . . . the *looks* on their faces—especially her boyfriends—of revulsion, horror, the *things* they said about her mother. One just said simple dumb stuff like, oh gross she's your *dad* that is fucked up, that is *fucked up*, and another said, hah, well, she was too pretty to actually be real anyway. *Hey* maybe he'll be a *penguin* next huh? though the worst was a girl, a close friend, who'd looked ashen then said: You know, it sucks, I knew she had problems but I still looked up to her as this strong woman. I thought I had this strong woman in my life. I thought you had this strong mother. Zoe clammed up about telling anyone after that, she didn't even mention it to Frankie. And so, when fall came and she applied for and squeaked into a fancy school on the East Coast, she saw for the first time in her town a void, endless black. She would be forever grateful she grew up there, but the future she saw was for some willowy gay kid, lovely but not her.

And then everyone's fucking attitudes about trans stuff changed so quickly after a few years. Chaz,

Thomas Beatie, all those fucks. Had she been born five years later, she thought sometimes, she might've felt like she could've stayed.

So. Zoe was bitter about that.

She looked away from her supervisor and adjusted her bag. I don't mind it, she said quietly. There's a lot of worse places to be.

Oh geez, said the supervisor, you have no idea! I *love* it here! He started talking about his hometown in Arizona and how there were grocery stores and bars here in Eugene he just loved and you'd never find that where he was from and just even the people were so nice, like, they gave a shit about being humans here, you know? He had grey eyes and they kind of sparkled as he talked. Zoe said uh-huh, totally, and decided to picture Al lubed and naked until they got to the bus station, where she returned some texts from Julia and the supervisor got on the 24 going somewhere south.

The next day Zoe was finishing cleaning the garage when Sandy walked up to Zoe from behind and hugged her and burrowed her head into Zoe's neck. Then Sandy said, I love that you're my daughter, and both of them shook and cried a little in the most delicious, healthy, loving of ways, the way that only mothers and daughters can. In a way that really, in a sense, Zoe had wanted to touch her mother for twenty-four years. They stood in the garage, cold, holding each other for a long time. She thought of Sandy's parents, estranged since before Sandy had even left home, and wondered fleetingly if it was possible to love so fully, as Sandy had, unless you had been cut off at some point from that love yourself.

She texted Frankie as she was going to work: *Hey Frankie. This is Zoe Quist. I had a different first name in high school, though you can probably figure out who this is anyway. I heard you're going through a tough time. If there's anything I can do please know you can call me. Or if you just want to hang out, that'd be nice too.*

The next evening she went to the bar with Robin and one of his lady friends. Zoe had a couple and went to shake it on the floor. She felt loose and free, in a rare silly mood. After a few songs a bro started creeping on her, dancing up close and touching her sides, her ass. She turned and gave a come-hither smile for half a second—the dude's smirk lit up—then she scrunched her face and shook both her head and forefinger. The dude scowled and went away. Zoe laughed and decided to get a third highball. The bar was crowded. A guy in a Crass shirt reached out his arm and started running his fingers through her hair. She smiled seductively at him too then took his hand and placed it on his chest. *No*, she enunciated.

I just like your hair! the guy hollered.

That's great, honey! Zoe said, smiling. You're not going to touch it! Nice shirt though!

Well give me a hug then! he said. Zoe laughed and did the smile-scrunch-head-and-finger-shake thing again. The guy's face crumpled in confusion. You'll say you like my shirt but you won't hug me? he said.

What can I say! Zoe yelled as the music got louder. It's a rough life!

Growing up Zoe was pretty deferent around boys, but a few months after the Williamsburg bar-owner-guy she started taking some pleasure out of messing with them like this.

A space at the bar opened. She shoved against it to flag down Al.

Zoe! said Al.

She smiled. *Zoe!*

Rum and diet? he asked.

No actually! she said. Gimme a G and T!

You got it!

She watched him pour. It was strong. She sipped the drink and tipped him big and said thanks!

Yeah!

He lingered in front of her for a second. She felt a

glow surge to her face. Hey! she said. I know you're at work and all so this is weird but—Al grinned and nodded hard and one of his curls fell into his face—do you want to hang out some time?

He hesitated. He didn't turn his head but she could see his eyes dart from side to side. Then he said sure! Can I find you on Facebook?

Sure! she said. Then she said you know what, actually no, fuck that! Fuck Facebook in its motherfucking penis! Gimme a pen! Al obliged. She took his forearm and on the inside steadily wrote her number in small script, ink shiny against the fish-white underbelly of his skin. There! she said. Call me when you want? I'll wait. Al smiled and then the guy in the Crass shirt yelled for beer.

Later, much later, Zoe and Robin and Robin's lady friend were coming out of the bar veering in the direction of Robin's house. The rain was the lightest of mist and none of them put their hoods up. She looked at a text from her mom (*KID I AM SO STONED*) and she giggled. Like oh, oh, this life. Zoe saw the hot dog cart on Olive and Broadway and snorted and said look at that shit.

What? Robin said.

A hot dog cart in Eugene! she laughed. Robin and the lady friend looked at her with blank drunkenness.

Zoe felt her phone go off and looked at a text: *Hey! This is Al! Now you have my number! Let's hang soon.*

She smiled big and toothy at her phone and they crossed the street and a man with coal fingernails and missing teeth came up to them, pulling down a home-made bandage to reveal a thick unbleeding open wound. Hey! he said. Do you maybe have some money for some beer, this tweaker bitch just stabbed me! He was smiling as if it had happened to somebody he didn't like. Robin and the lady friend's faces went glossy and said no, no sorry man, and Zoe's face crinkled and she said holy shit that sucks, yeah, hold on. She opened her wallet and took out her only bill, a five. Here you go man I hope—

Thank you! the man said, then continued and said, seriously, it was for *no* reason, she was *just a cunt you know, my God she was just a fucking CUNT YOU FUCKING! CUNT!* and went back to the curb where Zoe caught a glimpse of Al outside the bar, smoking a cigarette and peering at her standing in the middle of Olive Street, with her friends frozen and blinking a block behind her and her wallet hanging open like an unattended lip.

As Zoe lay passed out and cold on Robin's couch, Julia made her phone light and buzz through the night:

03:16: *Hey lady, woke up for work right now yr probably sleeping but I wish you were still here <3*

03:26: *Milton and me talking last night how we miss you a lot, like really miss you. We had Thanksgiving other week and propped up a pic of you on the table. We kept telling you to shut up. Good times*

03:59: *Ugh I hate the fucking subway. I wish you were here with me gorgeous you could clear the path haha*

04:14: *P.S. Lost your address and I wrote you post-cards!! send again?*

The next morning Robin's lady friend gave Zoe a ride home. She slouched against the window the entire ride north. She felt sick. Fuck, she had promised to help her mom this morning. And really—she felt bad about being so teasy to the guy in the Crass shirt (though fuck the bro who groped her). *Classy*, she thought darkly about the whole sexy-smile-scrunch-finger-wave thing. *Classy classy classy.* And then, *you can be nicer. There isn't always harm in being nicer.*

Hey party animal, Sandy said when Zoe walked in. She was at the kitchen table eating some grainy cereal with strawberries in it. Zoe tried to open the fridge and take out the milk.

No, no, Zoe said desperately.

You're hungover, huh, Sandy said. She looked tired and pissed.

I'm sorry. I'm sorry. What do we need to do today? Zoe said. She set the milk jug on the table with a thump and tried to sit down, but when the chair stopped her body's descent, her head kept going south and she face-planted in slow-motion on the tablecloth. Fuck, she said.

Sandy got up from the table. Jesus Christ, she said. Stay right there.

Okay, Zoe said into the tablecloth.

Sandy came back with four ibuprofen and a tall glass of water. Take these and drink all of this, she said.

Zoe obliged then said what do we need to do today?

Well first you're going to sleep for an hour, Sandy said. And no more.

Zoe stood up and made visibly strained efforts to stay vertical. I'll be fine, she said. I'm sorry, just. Gimme. A few minutes, I'll be fine.

Kid. Stop, said Sandy. You're going to bed. I am setting my alarm for an hour from now and then you may help me.

Zoe blinked and somehow stumbled without moving her feet.

When she was little, Zoe had nightmares; she had them all through childhood and far into adolescence, and before Sandy began falling asleep earlier than her, if Sandy heard Zoe thrashing, as Zoe often did, Sandy would come into her room and sing. She usually sang the mockingbird song, *Hush little baby don't say a word*—but sometimes, especially if Zoe was crying, Sandy would sing, *I'll love you forever, I'll like you for always, as long as I'm living, my baby you'll be.*

Zoe still had nightmares, though not quite as often. But she had one this morning where she was on the ground in a basketball court and a man was running at her from a long way to get at her and hurt her, he had two hands with long knives, three, four-foot long knives, and there was a car she could get to but her legs couldn't move and she couldn't—

ZOE!

Zoe's feet kicked the wall as she was shocked awake.

Yeah? she called out.

Hey! yelled Sandy from the living room. You've snoozed long enough, huh? I let you go 'til noon! Now come help me!

Zoe rubbed her eyes and searched for her bra and yelled coming! then rushed out her bedroom door.

Her mother's face softened when Zoe stumbled in and she said, you should eat something before we start.

No.

They opened the boxes Sandy'd taken down and started sorting. They made piles of stuff to keep or throw away or give to Goodwill. It wasn't exactly fun. Besides being hungover and ferociously hungry, everything Zoe saw just made her sad: Christmas-gift sweaters with moth holes in them, pictures of Sandy's birth fam that Sandy cut to pieces without pausing, a pretty and sheer yellow blouse Zoe reached to keep for herself when Sandy balled it and said this is like a whore-uniform from the fifties, what was I thinking.

They came across a few old pictures of Taya, and Sandy looked at them moodily then said so, you should keep these, and turned them face down and slid them toward Zoe on the floor. Zoe did like that. She and Taya'd never been close—probably wouldn't ever be, really—but she liked seeing pictures of her, especially from when Zoe was a kid.

When they were done, Zoe took the car to drop stuff off at Goodwill. She saw a woman there pawing through jeans with marks under her eyes dark as football paint. It made her think of Frankie, who hadn't gotten back to her. She wondered if maybe her number was different now so she texted Robin and said *Hey can you give me Frankie's number?*

He texted back as she was pulling out. *I can, sure, but why?*

I'll tell you later?

He did and the number was different so she retyped the same message and sent it. *There*, she thought. The rain got stronger as she drove home and became one of those true downpours that happened only every few weeks or so, a car-wash-grade spray that slowed every vehicle's speed by fifteen and turned everything from damp to just plain soggy. Back at the house, she bundled her coat and put on knee-high boots and went to ask her mom for a ride, but she had started day drinking—Sandy did that sometimes—so Zoe trudged down to the 66 and by the time the bus came every move she made was a squelch.

*

Months after she graduated college, four years into living in New York, Zoe had called her mother to tell her she had been on hormones for a while, that she was a girl, and, well, that that was that. Sandy'd made a high choking sound then said oh no.

A beat went by and Zoe said oh no?

Well what do you think, huh!? Sandy yelled. That's *that*, you think it's like you get a job or a boy or something?!?! Zoe made a choking noise of her own and then they were both silent for a long period in phone time, like twenty-five seconds, and then Sandy said, I'm sorry. I'm sorry. I'm sorry. You know what, I'm sure you want to talk. I know you want to talk. But I can't do this now, you'll need to give me some time.

Mom, Zoe said. I'm sorry.

I always wondered, Sandy said quietly, after another,

shorter, silence. So hey, there she be. But you'll need to give me a few weeks on this, kid.

Okay, Zoe said. I can do that. I'm sorry.

Kid, Sandy'd said. No apologizing. No apologizing. I can tell you that right now.

Okay.

They were silent some more and Sandy said yup, I'm gonna go. Don't call me for a while.

Okay.

Then Sandy said, well actually, hey.

Yes?

What's your name? Sandy asked.

It took her a few seconds to understand the question.

Zoe, she said. My name's Zoe.

That was when Sandy'd started crying, heavily. Okay, Zoe had said, sitting on her bed with a hand on her face. Sandy hung up. The thing with the Williamsburg bar owner had happened a week after that. Sandy didn't call her back for months. It hadn't been that great a time.

*

Do you work today? Sandy asked the next morning.

Yeah, at four.

Well, she said. After I go for a swim, I was going to

go to the mall and get some new clothes. Do you want to come with me? Get you, I dunno, a new shirt or something?

Oh sure! That'd be great! Zoe said. The two of them hadn't gotten out of the house together much.

Great, said Sandy. Maybe you can help me out with a new pair of jeans. I may actually get something with color today.

What? Sounds like an *abomination!* Zoe said. Sandy laughed and gave her a little slap on the shoulder and went out the door. Old joke. Once in middle school they'd been out with Sandy's girlfriend at the mall, and a woman with her husband saw Sandy and the girlfriend holding hands and cartoonishly loud whispered to him, an abomination I *tell* you. So for a few years everything was an abomination. Mom, can I have some Nutella? *What? ABOMINATION!* Hey kid, how do you feel about a movie tonight? *MOVIES! ABOMINATIONS!*

Later, in the car, Sandy said so. You know it's different now that there's two of us.

What do you mean?

You really not know what I mean?

Zoe sighed. Mom, I do not know what you mean, so why don't you just explicitly tell me what you mean.

Oh, well, I . . . Sandy muttered, oddly flustered all

of a sudden. You just—you tend to get more trouble in groups, that's all.

What?

Don't you know that?

Oh, said Zoe, well yeah I read that somewhere once but I didn't really—

Dammit it's true, Sandy said, suddenly aggravated. And I'm glad we're out doing stuff but Zoe, you can't be so cavalier. You can't.

The sky was breaking outside and cylinders of sunlight were lighting up mist like specks of silver. Sandy said, you can't just sail through the world all charmed and oblivious anymore, alright? It sounds depressing but it's true, *alright?*

Mom I do okay, Zoe said, feeling tiny.

Sandy concentrated on traffic but she looked pissed. Zoe stayed quiet.

Being pretty won't always protect you, said Sandy.

Zoe looked out the window. Stop it, Mom.

I'm serious! said Sandy. They'll find out you used to be a man!

Mom! Zoe cried. I don't! Want! To have this conversation! And I was never a *fucking man*, okay?

Sandy snort-laughed then she choked. Then she laughed kinda unable to breathe for a few seconds: *A-ha! A-ha! A-ha!* She sounded like she was trying to pass something. Ohhhh my *God! You* think you just stopped being my son, don't you? she said. Do you think that's how it works?! Do you think you went to a fucking wizard?!

Zoe put a hand in her hair and her other hand over her eyes. And Sandy said c'mon, tell me more, kid. She reached out her arm and pushed her daughter's left cheek like she was trying to wipe something on it. No! Zoe said. I don't! And Sandy said come on! Look. I'm here, aren't I?! Sandy went on like that for a bit and Zoe said no Mom, stop, just stop, then they got to the mall and out of the car.

The sun was still glinting through sky-cracks and the few people in the mall didn't give either woman much of a glance.

Zoe never got those kinds of glances, actually. Body-wise she'd been born as lucky as a lot of trans women would've ever hoped: She was tall but not Amazon-tall, had slight bones, narrow shoulders, a naturally high voice and only a hint of an Adam's apple. Her facial hair was blonde and even before electro never cast much of a shadow. She'd waited 'til she was ten months on hormones to go full-time, and she had never heard an unkind word in her direction about it. Not one episode of street harassment or threat. The trans variety, anyway. There were a few months where people stared like they weren't sure what was up, and she was mute in public for a little while, but that was it. She was

194

lucky, she knew it; none of her friends back in New York (like Julia, fuck . . .) could say that. But she'd more or less passed from the moment she wanted to.

They were silent in the mall as they walked to a clothing store. A man with a neatly trimmed beard smiled at Zoe and said to Sandy: Ma'am, if you don't mind me saying so, you have a beautiful daughter. Sandy flushed and said well thank you.

Sandy and Zoe were looking at jeans—Zoe generally wrinkled her nose at pants, but her one pair of black jeans was falling apart—when a clerk walked up and made a clearing noise in his throat and Sandy looked up unblinkingly and said yes?

Um. Can I help you, said the clerk.

No, my daughter and I are just fine thank you, she said curtly.

The clerk stared without responding for a couple seconds. Then he said yes, yes, of course.

In the dressing room, unzipping her skirt and sliding her hands down inside her tights, Zoe remembered when she'd told her mother she liked boys. She was thirteen. Though she'd been raised by lesbians, Zoe'd been nervous. She had imagined Sandy stormily yelling oh, so now *you* want to be different *too*, huh? or maybe saying, Lord, they were right, they all said it would end up like this . . . or maybe, she'd thought, Sandy would just slap her. Sandy was generally pretty hands-off but she had slapped Zoe a couple times. Once she'd thrown a video game controller at her.

But Sandy hadn't done anything like that, and she'd even appeared to be in one of her bad moods at the time. Immediately she'd smiled, as if something glistening had been poured on her face, and she opened her arms and said, I love you. Come here. She hugged Zoe tightly and said well, what do you know, you're one of us. Isn't that just the greatest.

On the ride home from the mall, Sandy started on how Zoe's tits were falling out of her shirt. Zoe tuned her out and stared out the window as her mother got going again, and didn't look back at her, not once, not even when Sandy screamed *LOOK AT ME* and dug her nails into Zoe's thigh.

Right before work ended that night Zoe texted Al: *Are you busy tonight? Would you want to hang out?*

She put her cell away and made one last call that devolved into arguing about the farm bill with a man outside Rickreall. She was about to leave the building when Al texted back. *Hey lady! Yes I do! I'm off in an hour, meet me at the Horsehead?*

Zoe groaned. Another fucking bar. She really was drinking way too much here. Oh well. The guy was a bartender and all.

As she walked down Olive she saw a homeless girl who looked like Frankie. It wasn't her, Zoe was pretty sure—well, but how could she know, she supposed, she hadn't seen Frankie in so long. Was it her? No, it didn't look like her. The hair was wrong and her eyes were a different color—maybe? It really could've been her. Zoe passed the girl and gave her a dollar. *No*, she thought, *it probably wasn't her*.

The mist coming down strengthened into steady rain and Zoe put her hood up.

OOGA-BOOGA! said her supervisor.

AH! Zoe wheeled around. She noticed for the first time that he had an arm tattoo of a kraken.

Sorry! he said, looking embarrassed. I didn't mean to scare you. Um, hey there. He put his hand on her shoulder and she shivered and shrugged it off.

There was an awkward couple seconds then she said where are you going?

Jameson's, he said. You?

Horsehead.

Oh so we're going the same way. Let's walk together!

Zoe thought of pointing out that both bars were exactly a block away then thought better of it. They walked over and parted ways and she went inside and ordered a Diet Coke. There. She didn't even *have* to be drinking in a bar.

She sat in the corner and took out her book. No

one bothered her. She had learned a default public bitch face in New York and she still had it, which honestly she didn't really like. She had liked living there, but she'd picked up some habits of hardness, too, that she wished she could give back.

Then Al was in front of her plunking down a PBR. Hey! How's it going, lady?

Great! Zoe put her elbows on the table and propped up her head with her fists. How are *you!*

Awesome awesome. Wow—damn. I haven't actually talked to you in a really long time! Al said. You were in New York, right?

Yeah! Brooklyn.

Okay, I've been wanting to say this since I saw you again. But not while I'm working, because that's creepy, right? But you look *really* good. Like, you look fuckin' *hot*. Shit can I say that? Is that okay? Like fuck, dude, good job.

Thanks, she blushed, thanks you're very nice.

Hey, don't thank me, speak truth to beauty, right? So what made you leave New York?

Uh, I was broke. And my mom needed help moving to Seattle for her new job. And all my shit was here. And I was broke.

I hear it's just a little expensive out there.

A month's rent here is like a . . . bag of apples over there. Or something.

Mmm. So tell me, you been the belle of every ball since you came back?

She scooched closer to the table. Oh pray tell what does *that* mean?

Come on lady, he grinned, you were el fuego at my bar the other night.

Oh please, that was, like, my one night off my butt. I'm really boring. Look. She picked up her drink. Diet Coke. I am the janitor of every ball, I am the DD of every ball.

Oh whatever, stop that! Al said. I don't believe that for a second! He said it in that weird way guys can that sounds mean and protective and attractive all at once. Then he softened and said, I'm sorry, I get it, I'm sure dating's really hard for you, I can't imagine.

Zoe blinked and said it's not actually—well, whatever. What about you?

Well, he smiled sheepishly, actually I've been meaning to say—I can only hang for so long, I have a date in a couple hours.

Ah, said Zoe. Yeah no problem. *Goddammit.* He nodded and she nodded for far too long and then she said a date at midnight? The fuck are you going to go, Shari's?

She works at DoughCo, he said.

Got it. She smiled. I think you should go to Shari's. $3.99 pie, mm-mm! The bathrooms are good for

blowjobs too, I'll bet you'll have a great time! She was
trying to laugh and sound cheery and silly but it really
wasn't working.

Uhhh I'm sure, Al said, taken aback.

What, don't you like blowjobs? She tried to laugh
again but she just sounded like a bird.

Uhhhhhhh, he said. Then his face made a tic and
his eyes lit up, then fell into something soft and kind.
And pitying. Oh . . . he said. You didn't think—

Mildly contrary to the upbringing she'd had, as
well as the neighborhood in Brooklyn where she'd spent
the last few years of her life, Zoe had never wanted to
live even a little bit wild. Her natural state was to wake
at seven and be reading in bed by ten, and her lifetime
ratio of cups-of-milk to units-of-booze was probably
around fifteen-to-one. She liked it that way. She definitely wasn't boring, you could never call Zoe that—she
loved to travel, she liked sex in quantities mass and frequent, she read books others pondered cracking and
when she made the time she sewed beautiful clothing
from scratch. But wild she wasn't. Whether it was here
or Brooklyn she had only ever wanted a few rooms and
a sweet dependable guy and, like, some plants. Shit job,
loud dirty town, rainy town, whatever, all of that could
be fine, she never minded, she just wanted the indoor
regular shelter of a nice dumb quiet life, not boring, just
quiet. When she'd grown up she'd thought it was here

and then she thought it was Brooklyn and now she thought it might be here again. So as much as her vision had blanked with disappointment, and as she briefly envisioned unquiet reactions—taking a bunch of shots, going across the street to her supervisor, just kissing Al anyway, fuck it—she knew she wasn't that kind of person. Not in the least. She was just going to say sorry, no, don't be silly! Of course not! It's okay. Sorry, I was being weird, I was being really weird just then. And she smiled politely and listened to Al talk about his girl then took the last bus home when he left. *It's funny*, she brooded, face pressed at the window looking over Coburg Road, her vision travelling the dark-dark-neon-dark pattern of closed stores and parking lots, the Dari-Mart, the Trader Joe's, the Albertsons, the Dairy Queen, the Burrito Amigos, the closed American Family Video, the Safeway and the Papa's Pizza and her old dentist's office, *it's only when they reject you that it really sinks in just how much you liked them.* She walked up Gilham and the sky was rainless with thin clouds scrum-lit in front of the moon; when she turned onto Ayers the rain returned again and the moon turned opaque, into a soft faraway light, as if covered by quilts. She entered the house and put the chips and salsa away from where Sandy had left them on the counter. She wiped the pot ash off too, then scrubbed off her makeup. She changed into pajamas and poured a glass of water in the kitchen, then noticed the saucepan sitting on the stove with crusts of hardened oatmeal rimming the sides and bottom. She looked at it for a long time then laid it quietly in the sink and filled it up with water.

Hey Taya! said Zoe when she opened her phone.

Yeah hello! said Taya. Well? How the heck are you?

It was far enough into December now that the trees were bare, and Zoe was raking the last leaves on the lawn. It was raining steadily and when a car sped past over on Gilham the water it kicked up looked like smoke. She put the rake down and sat on the front steps of the house.

Well, I'm getting rained on! said Zoe. How are you?

Getting sunned. Come to California.

I'd like to soon, Zoe said, I really would.

You probably wanna go back to New York though huh, Taya said.

Maybe.

How's Sandy? Taya asked.

She's great. She's just great. About to go to Seattle. How's the beau? she asked. Zoe always called Taya's boyfriends beaus. She started playing with the rake.

He's good, Taya said, lots of new clients. We're trying to set up a home office dealio at the moment but we need a bigger house.

Ah. Well, that sounds tough, Zoe said blankly. She tried spearing a single leaf without getting any others on the tines.

So any boys I should know about? Taya said.

Zoe rolled her eyes and said you can't see it but I'm rolling my eyes. Taya tittered.

Thought of you when I got this new dress yesterday, Taya said after a silence. It's lime green and has polka-dots on it and I just thought ooh, Zoe would love this, this is a *Zoe* dress.

Cool, Zoe said. She tried to turn around the rake to position it so she could remove the leaf with her teeth.

Well, it's good to talk with you, said Taya. Please keep in touch!

Sure, Zoe said. They hung up and she had a singular text from Julia: *Woman! Where are you? Yr killing me!*

*

Robin and Zoe were eating at Burrito Boy after Zoe got off work. So what're we doing tonight? said Robin.

Can we please not go to the bar? Zoe said.

Tall order, said Robin.

Well we can, she said. I just don't want to be there for long. Like one drink?

Robin said yeah. There's a girl I wanted to say hi to

there. How about we go quick, and we'll be out of there in an hour. An hour cool?

Sure, Zoe said quickly. Even if it ends up being more than an hour, just, like, promise me we'll end up back at your place early enough to watch a dumb movie and be in pajamas and stuff? Please?

Promise.

When they got to the bar, Zoe's supervisor was there. He came up and chatted with her and Robin then bought a round of shots for the table. He was young to have grey hair, Zoe thought, couldn't be past his early thirties. Beyond the kraken tattoo on his arm Zoe noticed another one, near his shoulder, of a boy reading on a floor. She liked that. Then he excused himself to the dance floor and said hey hey, join anybody?

Zoe made a weighing motion with her hands and gave him a cute smile, then sucked on her rum and diet. The supervisor blew kisses at them both and went to dance.

Hey, she said to Robin, does he know about me?

Robin immediately shook his head. No. If he does, I didn't tell him.

Thanks, she said. You're a good friend.

Robin smiled happily and said it's none of his business!

That's right, she said.

Robin went to the bathroom and Zoe watched the

supervisor on the floor. *Someone overlearned 'dance like no one's watching,'* she thought. His eyes were half-closed and his limbs were kicking everywhere and he had a chunk of the floor to himself pretty quick. Zoe sat and watched him for a whole song. She liked watching men in moments like this. Like they were both self-possessed and not.

She went to the floor and tapped him on the shoulder. He turned around and Zoe made some jazz hands. The supervisor laughed. He was drunk. He hugged Zoe and they danced for a couple songs. Then Zoe said hey, let's, like, talk. Outside. He put on a serious face and said yeah, sure, hey, whatever you need, you know.

Zoe led him around the corner and behind Lazar's Bazaar then turned him and kissed him; she kissed him for what she figured was a minimum pretense of time and then dropped her hand into his waistband and then she was kneeling with her back against a chain link fence. It was raining the lightest of mists again and she latently felt her hair gradually turn from dry to not dry to damp. She sucked him methodically, quick, almost mechanically but not in an unpleasurable way. After a couple minutes she took him down to the base and then pushed on his behind to guide him a bit; he started fucking her mouth and she made sounds to signal *Yes! Good!* though who knows if he really heard or paid attention to them or what. After he came she hugged him, same position, her arms wrapped around his legs and his emptied cock in her throat, breathing in through the nose, out through the nose, in through the nose, out through the nose, in through the nose, out thro—

—he slipped himself out and she almost fell forward from leaning.

He helped her up and hugged her and tried to finger her but she'd already locked her thighs tight. Kiss me, she said. Kiss me. Kiss me. They kissed and kissed and she touched his face all over, and in a smooth motion he lifted her hands up and leaned her back against the fence while pulling his body close to hers. She wasn't expecting it and he was smiling and then he stopped smiling and said oh.

Zoe flinched and pivoted and took a step back, then she poised, she was ready to run or scream but she was too tipsy and tired to feel fear, really, she was more just weary, defensive. Like, okay. So. Now this is a thing that's going to happen. I guess I could've seen that coming. But then he just put on a stupid smile and made a stupid little laugh and said haha in a tinny voice and then said well I guess I'll see you at work soon.

An hour and a few drinks later Robin said sorry I took longer. Let's go?

The weather turned nasty when they left the bar,

another rare heavy spray. They both only had hoodies and then Zoe gave hers to a shivering dude with a soggy cardboard sign—she had a job now, whatever—so she was especially cold but soon they were both at underwear-squelch level anyway so it didn't really matter.

Fuck Oregon! she yelled over the sound of the rain.

Yeah! Robin yelled back. Fuck this fucking state!

I don't ever want to see water again!

Let's live on milk! he hollered.

Now you're talking!

After twenty minutes they got to Robin's place and Zoe found out the pajamas in her bag had gotten wet. Shit, she said, showing him as he shucked off his clothes. Can I borrow something to sleep in? Robin said sure and went to his room.

An oversized band T-shirt and grey billowy mesh shorts sailed into the living room and landed on the couch. She eyed them; they were faded and threadbare, she actually remembered Robin wearing both these things in high school. She changed in the bathroom with her back to the mirror. Back in the kitchen she heated up warm milk for the two of them. You'll like it, she found herself saying. Sssh! Just let it happen, let it happen, she said, and at that Robin laughed.

Hey, Ye Olde Supervisor really seemed to like you, he said. He hadn't noticed them stepping out, he'd been talking to that girl and he only saw that the two of them had been dancing.

Yeah, he seems like a nice guy, Zoe said. Don't think that one's a good idea though.

Oh right, of course not, duh, he said, tapping himself on the head. Work boss relationship. Thing.

Then he said hey, speaking of that, I know it must be tough for you with, like, dating and all. So, uh . . .

Mmmmm? Zoe said.

Robin's upper teeth appeared to rest on his lower lip. Well, he said, I know this dude who wants to go on a date with you. If you wanted me to set you up. He's seen you at the bar and stuff, he asked me if you were single.

Sure, Zoe said blandly.

I don't know if you'll like him, he said quickly. I don't know if *I* like him, but I figure maybe it's hard for you to find guys and I know he's into girls like you and so maybe it's not my place and I should just connect you with him anyway.

Do it, give him my number, she said, shaking the saucepan a little. She didn't look at him. I really don't care.

Okay, cool, Robin said hurriedly. I just have to say that, you know, for my own conscience, but like I said maybe it's not my place.

It's okay, Zoe said, pouring the milk and beckoning

him into the bedroom. They sat on his bed shaking off the chill, and as she watched him close his eyes to drink—he had such long, pretty eyelashes—suddenly Zoe said you get nightmares a lot, don't you?

Sometimes, Robin said softly.

Aw, Zoe said, drawing a finger across his cheek. The rain was making bullet sounds against the air conditioner outside the window. She caught her reflection in his dresser mirror. The oversized T-shirt and shorts filled out and enlarged her little frame. Her eye flickered like she'd taken a swallow of something utilitarian, like cough syrup or bottom-shelf gin.

A childhood memory of her mother suddenly settled in her head, like a fallen balloon. In it she was dutifully standing by Sandy's desk as Sandy was crying and talking to her. She'd said a lot of things, but all Zoe remembered was Sandy saying *please don't ever look up to me*, and Zoe saying *okay*.

Nightmares of what? Zoe asked. Why? Robin closed his eyes and his long eyelashes fluttered a bit, and he shook his head and Zoe said you deserve something to make that better. She stroked his wavy brown hair.

You're a good friend, Robin said, curling away from her and lying on the bed, then swaddling himself in blankets. You're a good, good friend.

*

This is the last bit, Sandy said as they went down to the laundry nook of the basement. Once we get this corner cleared out, you're free. I release you.

Cool, said Zoe. I'll probably stick around 'til the weekend. If that's okay.

Do whatever you want, said Sandy. You know where you're going yet?

Zoe shrugged. Look for a place here? I guess? Robin knows a few people who need roommates. And it looks like I can crash on his couch until then.

Sandy scrunched her face like she was confused about a smell. You would hate that, wouldn't you?

Extremely, said Zoe. Can't be a princess all the time though.

I've been waiting years to hear you say that.

Shut up!

They cleaned the machines as best they could then started on the cabinet above the dryer. Hey, Sandy said thoughtfully. So I've seen you reconnect with some of your old friends here. Have you seen Frankie at all?

Funny you ask. Nobody really knows, actually, said Zoe. She picked up a leaking bottle of detergent with a logo she hadn't seen since high school and dropped it in the garbage. Oh my God Mom this is gross, she said. The sink needs to be on like right now.

Sandy turned on the hot water in the big industrial

sink and slime glided off Zoe's fingers. What do you mean, no one knows? said Sandy.

Well I know she had a kid.

Sandy blinked. What.

She gave it up for adoption is what I hear, but she fell off the map after that.

Oh my God, Sandy said.

Supposedly she's back here in town. I tried texting her, said Zoe. But she never responded. I'm worried though, I think I might've seen her on the streets the other day, like, panhandling.

What about her dad? Sandy said.

Oh fuck. I never told you. He died. Cancer.

Fuck, Sandy said, softer than her daughter.

Yeah. Then Zoe's face clouded and her tone turned mean. *Apparently*, she said, Frankie never even saw him while he was dying either, she just skipped out. *And* I heard she got really into coke too, I mean, Jesus.

So you're telling me, Sandy said, that one of your old friends who no longer has parents and just had a baby who she had to give up is possibly on the streets right now and possibly has problems with serious fucking drugs and all you did was text her.

Zoe was silent.

She could be dying, kid, Sandy said.

Zoe looked at the floor. I guess I just, she—

OH SHUT *UP!* Sandy said, throwing the detergent

bottle on the floor like she was spiking it. Zoe jumped and screamed, immediately scared. She backed against the wall and her mother continued: None of you get it around here! You don't know what friendship means! No, it could never mean life and death, could it? Humans aren't fucking games where you just try your best! Okay! Every night you've spent—she stopped and said, why am I about to waste time yelling. Let's get in the car.

Why are we getting in the car? said Zoe.

We're going to look for her.

Zoe's mouth opened and Sandy moved to the stairs. She ducked her head under the doorframe and put one of her wide, chapped hands on the railing, then glanced back at her daughter. The whites of Sandy's eyes were glossy and nicotine-yellow, and Zoe could see her calves tense on the first step with spider-web strands of pain. She was getting old.

That her mother could walk through the longest desert and keep walking was a thought that entered and exited Zoe's mind. We will find her? Zoe asked. Who knows, Sandy said. Let's get in the car.

When Zoe was little, like nine, a kid in her school had once said on the playground, your mom's a *man!* Don't you know your mom's a *man!* My dad told me, he told me everything, you're not even homos you're like freaks for homos. He was a strong kid, an older kid, and he used to slap Zoe, not really hard, he just did it a lot, around the face and arms and sometimes in the nuts. He went on the whole your-mom's-a-man thing for a week and never said anything to the other kids or teachers, who knows why; maybe he figured no one would believe him. Zoe had told Sandy about it that weekend, a Saturday, and Sandy'd put her head in her hands and said what's the kid's name. Zoe told her and Sandy said his dad's name is Don, right. Huge guy. Loud guy. Zoe said yes, and Sandy said okay and left and was still gone when Zoe went to sleep, and the next day Sandy spent all day in bed and wouldn't talk to anyone, called in sick the next day and stayed in her room again though she called Zoe in before school to kiss her on the head, and Zoe could hear her moving around when she left the house and at school the kid wasn't bothering Zoe anymore and then on Tuesday Sandy got up and went back to work.

Zoe was still in the basement as Sandy stopped for breath on the stairs. Then she shook something final out of her body, and followed her mother up.

Gunk

by Irenosen Okojie

Gunk is a term in mereology for any whole whose parts all have further proper parts.

Get up. Try to hold your world. You can't. You let it slip. I know your world; car horns, aspiration, language, screaming traffic lights, spies. I see you. Your thick hair is overgrown, run an afro comb through it. Your wiry frame is still poised to move in sleep, to change shape at the edges of iodine-stained misfortunes. I showed you how to plant, how to sow seeds in concrete, yet your seeds don't grow. I demonstrated ways to sheathe knives in skin, yet you only injure yourself. Boy, you don't fly. You don't appreciate flight. You just want to prove what a waste of space you are.

Stop trembling in the fucking corner. Don't pick up that medicine. They numb you, sedate you, curtail your potential. Don't follow the script. You weren't designed for this.

It's a set up. The system is fucking rigged. Your enemies plotted against you, danced on platforms in the sky, taunted you with disguises, reached into the chests of people you used to know. You rage because this city has broken you. This world has sucked your resolve through a pit. You rage because everything is a lie. Choice is an illusion. Its sibling conformity met you at the airport. Boy, you stepped into his fucking embrace proving what a waste of space you are. His smile made you forget your mother tongue while she battled the elements on your behalf, changing gears on any given day.

Remember Corrine? You told her coffee skin your secrets. She laughed, curved her wide mouth down to catch. You buried your face in her afro, travelled through it. You destroyed each other then came up for air. You watched her fly down the street engulfed in blue flames. A small universe spilled from her bag; notebook, pen, Vaseline, keys, items to trace on the scratched table when fear arrived with some creature's hind legs.

Your pity stinks. Stop cowering in the corner. Stop crawling naked on top of that wardrobe. You can't reinvent yourself from contained heights.

Darkness motivates men, mobilises armies. Use it. You are a warrior. Show me your roar. People are scared of your power, frightened of what you can do with it.

Once you wanted to be an engineer. Instead, those dreams drowned in the Thames. Instead, you walked off construction sites breathing sawdust. Instead, you avoided eye contact more so than usual. Instead, you resisted the urge to carry your internally bleeding head on public transport.

Follow my lead. Use those memories as lamps to see through your rooms. Nobody cares here. Footsteps on the stairs outside don't pause at this door. The carnival whistle hanging on the dented hallway wall waits for a cry that left you at birth to fill it. Your mobile phone stopped ringing. It's just you and me. You don't have any tricks. You just keep showing what a waste of space you are. You want to pick up that old taekwondo trophy and smash me to pieces. You can't. I gave you DNA.

These extras we programme ourselves to think are necessary—family, friends, jobs, love, companionship—these sentiments weakening us only serve as cushions to soften the inevitable blow. You'll die one day. Look around you, this is really it. Scraping pennies together so often it's become a past time, rummaging for money inside the sofa. Cracks in the ceiling, the floor that's turned to quicksand. No cash to charge the electricity, your fridge door opening to reveal half a yoghurt, one-day-old kebab. This unending humiliation of you to yourself facilitates nothing.

The couple next door were once in love. Now, you hear plates smashing, arguments fuelled by alcohol, the ripping of each other's carcasses, their misguided notions of loyalty. You watch their ugly Bombay cat skulking outside trying to trace where it pissed over the remedy for doomed lovers rising through cold soil.

You sit by this window looking out, hoping for answers. Boy, I gave you answers. If you weren't so busy showing what a waste of space you are, you'd remember. Your enemies are everywhere. They want to destroy you with fear. Don't let them do it. Don't be a puppet. I taught you better. I showed you better. I schooled you better. Don't be a victim. This is what a victim looks like. This is what you look like. Don't look like that. Didn't I teach you how they operate? Didn't I tell you how you're conditioned? Don't swallow what they're shoving down your throat. It costs them nothing. Didn't I teach you about currencies that can't be seen with the naked eye? Yet there you go proving what a waste of space you are.

Are you a small country? Are you a fucking island? Don't let your enemies conquer you. Don't let them limit you. Don't let them gag you. Don't let them buy your cooperation with their sleight of hand. Didn't I give you ammunition? Didn't we sharpen our tools? Didn't we aim for our bullseye from every possible angle, every feasible position? Yet there you lay trying to show what a waste of space you are. Don't make me transform. Don't make me reconfigure.

I carried you.

I bled for you.

I suffered for you.

Stay close to me, listen. Every word I say to you is true.

Fuck governments.

Fuck systems.

Fuck everything that tells you if you're good you'll
be valued.

Somebody always has to pay.

Make people pay.

We've paid enough.

Open your eyes. Get up from that bottom.

Son, this is the skin I'm leaving you with.

This is how to wear it comfortably.

This is how to camouflage when you need to.

This is how to start a war.

Remember: It's your world now.

Heaven

by Mary Gaitskill

When Virginia thought of their life in Florida, it was veiled by a blue-and-green tropical haze. Ocean water lapped a white sand beach. Starfish lay on the shore and lobsters awkwardly strolled it. There was a white house with a blue roof. On the front porch were tin cans housing smelly clams and crayfish that walked in circles, brushing the sides of the cans with their antennae; they had been brought by her son Charles, and left for him and his brother, Daniel, to squat over and watch from time to time.

She imagined her young daughters in matching red shorts, their blond hair pulled back by rubber bands. The muscles of their long legs throbbed as they jumped rope or chased each other, rubber thongs patting their small, dirty heels with every step. A family picnic was being held in the front yard on an old patchwork quilt. Watermelon juice ran down their sleeves.

Jarold was holding Magdalen in the ocean so she could kick and splash without fear. He was laughing, he was pink; his hair lay in wet ridges against his large, handsome head.

Twenty years later, Virginia thought of Florida with pained and superstitious but reverent wonder, as though it was a paradise she had forfeited without knowing it. She thought of it almost every night as she lay on the couch before the humming, fuzzing TV set in the den of their New Jersey home. She lay with her head on a hard little throw pillow, staring out of the picture window into the darkened back yard at the faint glimmer of the rusting barbecue tray. She thought that if they had stayed in Florida, her son would still be alive. She knew it didn't make any sense, but that's what she thought.

When Virginia met Lily, her fifteen-year-old niece, Lily had said to her, 'Grandmother used to tell us about you all the time. She said you could pick oranges in your back yard. She said you once found a lobster walking in your living room. She said there'd be tornadoes and your house would flood, and horrible snakes would come in. You sounded so exotic. It didn't seem like you could be related to us.'

They were riding in the warm car with their seat belts on. Virginia had just picked Lily up at the Newark airport because Lily was coming to live with them.

Virginia had been charmed by her remark.

*

Lily's mother was visiting Jarold and Virginia. It had been almost eight years since Virginia had spent so much time with her sister.

Anne was the short, brown-haired sister to two tall blondes, a nervous, pitifully conscientious child who always seemed to be ironing or washing or going off somewhere with an armload of books. Her small mouth was a serious line. Her large gray eyes were blank and dewy. She often looked as though she was about to walk into a wall.

Since Anne was the oldest by five years, their mother made her responsible for the care of Virginia and Betty on weekends, when she went into Lexington to clean houses for rich people. Anne accepted the responsibility with zeal. She rose early to get them eggs and milk for breakfast, she laid the table with exquisite care, wreathing the plates with chains of clover. Virginia and Betty complained when she dragged them out of bed to eat; they made fun of her neat breakfast rituals. They refused to help her with the dishes.

Anne dated only scholarly boys. She spent earnest, desperate hours on the porch with them, talking about life and holding hands. She'd bound up the stairs afterward, her eyes hotly intent, her face soft and blushing with pleasure. Her sisters would tease her, sometimes until she cried.

At forty-eight, Anne had become plump, homely

and assured. Her eyes had become shrouded with loose skin and she wore large beige glasses. Her eyebrows had gotten thick, but her pale skin was fine and youthful.

During the visit it was Anne who made charming, animated conversation with Jarold and Magdalen. It was she who laughed and made them laugh on the canoe trips and barbecues. Virginia sat darkly silent and meek, watching Anne with interest and some love. She knew Anne was being supportive. Anne had been told that Virginia had not recovered well from Charles's death, and had come to bring lightness to the darkened house. She was determined to cheer Virginia, just as she'd been determined to mop the floor or make them eat their breakfast.

She had approached Lily with the same unshakable desire to rectify.

Lily's presence in Virginia's life began as a series of late-night phone calls and wild letters from Anne. The letters were full of triple exclamation points, crazy dashes or dots instead of periods, violently underlined words and huge swirling capital letters with tails fanning across several lines. 'Lily is so withdrawn and depressed.' 'Lily is making some very *strange* friends.' 'Lily is hostile.' 'I think she may be taking drugs ...' 'Think she needs help – George is resisting – may need recommendation of a counselor.'

Virginia imagined the brat confronting her gentle sister. Another spoiled, pretty daughter who fancied herself a gypsy princess, barefooted, spangled with bright beads, breasts arrogantly unbound, cavalier in love. Like Magdalen.

'I want to marry Brian in a gypsy wedding,' said Magdalen. 'I want to have it on the ridge behind the house. Our friends will make a circle around us and chant. I'll be wearing a gown of raw silk with a light veil. And we'll have a feast.'

'Does Brian want to marry you?' asked Virginia dryly.

Magdalen was seventeen. She had just returned home after a year's absence. She carried a fat green knapsack on her back. Her feet were filthy. 'I'm coming home to clear my head out,' she said.

She ate huge breakfasts with eggs and bacon, baked a lot of banana bread and lay around the den playing with tarot cards. Family life went on around her brooding, cross-legged frame. Her long blond hair hung in her face. She flitted around with annoying grace, her jeans swishing the floor, humming songs about ladies on islands.

After six months she 'decided' to marry Brian, and went to Vancouver to tell him about it.

Virginia was glad to see her go. But, even when she was gone, insistent ghosts of Magdalen were everywhere: Magdalen at thirteen, sharp elbows on the breakfast table, slouching in an overlong cashmere sweater, her sulky lips ghoulish with thick white lipstick – 'Mom, don't be stupid, everybody wears it'; twelve-year-old Magdalen, radiant and triumphant, clutching an English paper graded triple A; Magdalen in the principal's office, her bony white legs locked at the ankle, her head primly cocked – 'You've got a bright little girl, Mrs Heathrow. She should be moved at least one year ahead, possibly two'; Magdalen lazily pushing the cart at the A&P, wearing yellow terry-cloth shorts and rubber sandals, her chin tilted and her green cat eyes cool as she noticed the stock boys staring at her; fifteen-year-old Magdalen, caught on the couch, her long limbs knotted up with those of a long-haired college freshman; Magdalen, silent at the dinner table, picking at her food, her fragile nostrils palpitating disdainfully; Magdalen acting like an idiot on drugs, clutching her mother's legs and moaning, 'Oh, David, David, please make love to me'; Magdalen in the psychiatrist's office, her slow white fingers dropping cigarette ashes on the floor; Jarold, his mouth like a piece of barbed wire, dragging a howling Magdalen up the stairs by her hair while Charles and Daniel watched, embarrassed and stricken.

For years Magdalen had overshadowed two splendid boys and her sister, Camille. Camille sat still for years, quietly watching the gaudy spectacle of her older sister. Then Magdalen ran away and Camille emerged, a gracefully narrow-shouldered, long-legged girl who wore her light-brown hair in a high, dancing ponytail. She was full of energy. She liked to wear tailored blouses and skirts, but in home economics she made herself a green-and-yellow snakeskin jumpsuit, and paraded around the house in it. She delighted her mother with her comments: 'When boys tell me I'm a prude, I say, "You're absolutely right. I cultivate it."' She was not particularly pretty, but her alert, candid gaze and visible intelligence made her more attractive than most pretty girls. When Virginia began to pay attention to Camille, she could not understand how she had allowed Magdalen to absorb her so completely. Still, there were ghosts.

Magdalen had been gone for over a year when Anne called. It was a late summer night. Virginia and Jarold were in the den watching *Cool Hand Luke* on TV. The room was softly dark, except for the wavering white TV light. The picture window was open. The cool night air was clouded with rustlings and insect noises. Virginia sat with her pink sweater loose around her shoulders, against Jarold's arm. Their drinks glimmered before them on the coffee table. Virginia's cigarette glowed in a metal ashtray. Their sparerib dinner had been lovely.

Charles called her to the phone, and she felt a thrill of duty. What had happened to Lily now? She took her drink and cigarettes and left the gentle darkness, padding down the hall and through the swing door into the kitchen. The light was bright and there was a peaceful smell of old food. She shooed Charles, who was eating a dish of lime sherbet at the counter, and sat on the high red stool under the phone, her elbows on her knees. 'What is it, honey?'

Lily had just been released from a mental hospital. 'All she does is lie around like a lump, eating butter sandwiches and drinking tea like a fiend. I don't think she can go back to school here, now that she's been expelled. We've already tried sending her away to school and that didn't work either. I don't know what to do.'

Magdalen was somewhere in Canada. Camille was away at college. Charles and Daniel were always outside playing. 'Why doesn't Lily come and go to school here?' she said. 'I'm fresh out of girls, you know. Send her on out.'

She went back into the den forty minutes later. Jarold was hunched forward on the couch with the exasperated expression that he always had when he was watching liberals on TV. He was so intent on *Cool Hand Luke* that he didn't ask about the telephone call. She cuddled against him silently.

She meant to tell him about Lily after the movie

228

was over, but she didn't. She planned to tell him for several days. Then she realized she was putting it off because she knew he would say no. So she decided not to tell him anything. All week, she fantasized about Lily, and what it would be like to have her there.

A week later, she picked Lily up at the airport. As she stood shielding her eyes to scan the passengers climbing from the plane, she realized that she had been vaguely expecting Lily to look like Magdalen. She felt a slight shock when she noticed the small, pale, brown-haired girl. Even as Virginia adjusted her expectation, she was surprised by Lily's appearance. She had not imagined such a serious face. As Lily came toward her among the passengers, Virginia felt an odd sense of aloneness about the girl. Her gray eyes were wide and penetrating, but seemed veiled, as if she wanted to look out without you looking in. Her mouth and jaw were stiff and rather pained. Virginia was curious and taken aback.

She bought Lily a can of grape pop and took her to the car. It was a humid day; the seats were sticky and hot. They rolled down all the windows, and Virginia turned on the radio to a rock station. Lily didn't say much until they got out on the turnpike. Then she said the thing about Florida. Virginia was surprised and pleased. She laughed and said, 'Well, we did chase a few lobsters around the house, but it would take more than that to make us exotic. We just couldn't manage to keep the doors and windows shut at the same time.'

'Maybe exotic isn't the right word,' said Lily. 'You were just so obviously different from us. Mother showed us pictures of you and you always seemed so self-assured. I remember a picture of Magdalen and Camille. They were both standing with their hips out and one of them – Magdalen, I guess – had her foot perched up on something. They looked so blond and confident.'

Virginia thought of the pictures she had seen of Anne's family. In a group, they looked huddled together and meek, even when they were all smiling brightly. They looked as though they were strangers to the world outside their family, as if they had come out blinking, wanting to show their love and happiness, holding it out like a shy present. Anne's daughters were pretty in a different way from Magdalen or Camille. She remembered a picture of Lily and her sister Dawn crouching in a sandbox in frilly red sunsuits. Their brown hair just reaching their shoulders, and the bashful smiles on their bright, thin lips seemed heartbreakingly, dangerously fragile to her.

'Well, you all looked darling to us,' she said. 'We could tell you were sweet as pie.'

Virginia left the highway and took Lily for a drive through the mountains. She drove to the top of a hill that looked down on a lake and some old dull-colored green pines. They were near a convent, and the woods were planted with white daisies and small purple flowers. They got out and walked until Virginia felt a light sweat on her skin. Then they sat on a stone bench near the convent and told each other family stories. Virginia liked Lily. She was intrigued by her. She wondered why such an intelligent child could not do well in school.

They went home and Virginia made them cups of tea.

Charles and Daniel came home from school. They were surprised to see Lily, and to hear that she was coming to live with them. They sat at the table and Virginia served them pieces of coconut cream pie. The three children had a short, polite conversation. Charles said, 'That's a cool knapsack. My sister Magdalen has one like that.'

When the boys went upstairs, Virginia began to worry. Jarold was coming home, and she still hadn't thought of what to say to him.

She decided to take a shower and put on a pretty blouse. She told Lily to make herself at home, and went upstairs. When she came down again, she found Jarold in the kitchen; he had left work early. He was standing at the table, his face red and bitterly drawn about the eyes. He looked at Virginia like she was his enemy. Lily looked at her too, her face stiff and puzzled. Jarold walked out of the room.

She and Jarold talked about it that night. Apart from the intrusion, Jarold did not like Lily. 'She's weird,' he said. 'She has no social graces. She just stares at you.' They were lying in bed on their backs in their summer pajamas, their arms lying away from their bodies in the heat. The electric fan was loud.

'Jarold, she's shy,' said Virginia. 'And she's upset. She's had a hard time these last few months.'

'Whose fault is that? Why do we have to get stuck with her hard time, Virginia? Answer me that.'

Virginia lay still and looked at her long naked feet standing at the end of the bed. She couldn't think of an answer.

'And she's got such a pasty little face,' continued Jarold. 'She looks like something that crawled out from under a rock.'

'Jerry.' Her voice was soft and blurry in the fan.

'I don't think Jarold likes me,' said Lily the next day.

Virginia was doing the dishes. Lily stood beside her, leaning against the wall, standing on one leg.

'He just needs time to get used to you.' Virginia dug around in the water for the silverware and tried to think of something to say. 'He told me last night that you remind him of Magdalen. And he loved Magdalen.'

Virginia could feel Lily brightening.

'But you see, Magdalen hurt him more than anyone else in the world. It's a painful memory for him.'

'I guess so,' said Lily. 'He told me I look like something that crawled out from under a rock.'

Jarold was a big, handsome man who sold insurance to companies. His handsomeness was masculine and severe. His bright blue eyes were harsh and direct, and his thin, arched eyebrows gave him an airy demon look that was out of character with his blunt, heavy voice. He rarely made excessive or clumsy movements, although his walk was a little plodding. He had become successful very quickly. They had never been forced to live in small apartments with peeling wallpaper. For years Virginia believed that Jarold could surmount anything. He could, too, until Magdalen.

Jarold had been in love with Magdalen. At breakfast, he would look at her as she sullenly pushed her egg around her plate while the other children chattered, as if her bored, pale face gave him the energy to go to work. He read all of her papers from school; he always wanted to take her picture. She could make him do anything for her. He'd let her stay out all night; he let her spend the weekend in New York when she was fifteen. Wherever she was, even when she was traveling around Canada with a busload of hippies and a black person, if she cabled home for money, Jarold sent it immediately. If he tried to be strict, she would tease and flatter him. The few times he lost his temper and punished her, she punished him with silence. When he dragged her up the stairs and spanked her, she ran away from home. She called a week later and spoke to Virginia, but she hung up when Jarold got on the phone. It was the first time that Virginia had seen Jarold cry.

'Magdalen has real charm,' said Jarold to Lily. 'She can charm the birds off the trees. You don't have any of that. You don't have any personality at all.'

Virginia was surprised at the intensity of Jarold's dislike for Lily. And, although Lily never expressed it openly, Virginia felt that Lily hated him too. Lily never argued with him; she barely acknowledged his presence. When she had to speak to him, her voice was clipped and subtly condescending, as though he were beneath defiance.

One evening, Lily and Virginia were sitting together in lawn chairs in the back yard when Charles and Daniel approached them with a big piece of wood. The boys had shot four squirrels, skinned them and nailed the skins to it. They displayed the skins proudly, and Virginia praised them. Lily said nothing until they left. Then she said that she thought it was sick.

'I know, it seems awful,' said Virginia. 'But they're little boys and it means something to them. They do it to impress their father.' Virginia was unnerved by the sudden look of contempt on Lily's face.

'I know,' she said.

Lily's stay gradually became more and more unpleasant and eventually became a discomfiting memory that hung over the house for quite a while. But there were bright spots that stood out of the unpleasantness so vividly that they seemed to come from somewhere else altogether.

Virginia would spend afternoons with Lily after school. They'd change into jeans and T-shirts and drive into the mountains where they'd gone the first day. Sometimes they'd stop at a Dairy Queen and buy pink-spotted cups of ice cream in melting puddles of syrup. They'd sit on the car hood, slowly swinging their legs and eating the ice cream with pink plastic spoons, talking about the bossy girl in Lily's home ec class, or the boy she thought was 'different.' Virginia spoke about her high school days, when she was beautiful and popular and all the girls tried to be friends with her. She'd give Lily social advice about how to choose her friends.

When they'd get to the mountains, they'd leave the car and walk. They'd become quiet and concentrate on the walk. They'd find paths, then break branches from trees and use them to clear their way. Lily would stop to examine plants or insects, her brow taut and puzzled. She'd pick up a lot of things to hold in her pockets, especially chestnuts. She would pick up a chestnut and hold it in her hand for the whole walk, stroking it with her fingers, or meditatively rubbing it across her lower lip.

Other times they'd just sit at the kitchen table and drink tea. Virginia was astonished at the things she told Lily during these afternoons. Lily knew things about Virginia that very few other people knew. Virginia did not know why she confided in her. She had been lonely. The afternoon kitchen was sunny and lulling. Lily listened intently. She asked questions. She asked a lot of questions about Magdalen.

'But don't you like Magdalen?' she asked once. 'Weren't there good times when she was growing up?'

'Magdalen could be the most lovely, charming child in the world – if she wanted to be. She'd give you the shirt off her back – if she was in the mood. *If* she was in the mood. But to answer your question, no, I don't like Magdalen. I love her – I love her dearly – because I'm her mother and I can't help it. But I don't like her.'

Lily stared at her, pale and troubled.

'Don't you ever repeat that. It's very private. If Magdalen ever comes to me and says, "Mama, Lily says you don't like me," I'll say you're lying.'

As they talked, Lily rested her elbow on a small pile of school-books. She carried these books to and from school every day. One of them had a split green cover that showed its gray cardboard stuffing and a dirty strip of masking tape running up its broken spine. Whenever Lily heard Jarold pull into the driveway, she would grab her books and leave the room. Jarold would come in and see her cup on the table, its faint sugary crust fresh around the bottom. He'd never say anything, but his mouth got sarcastic.

Virginia tried to get Jarold to be nicer to Lily. 'She's got a special kind of charm,' she said. 'She's gentle and low-key. She listens, and she has fresh insights.' Sometimes Jarold looked as though he were listening to this.

But Lily wouldn't or couldn't show Jarold her charm. To him, she displayed only her most annoying aspects. And they really were annoying. She almost never said anything at family meals; she either kept her head down and chewed, or stared at people. She ignored Jarold, and sometimes she ignored Virginia too. She was judgmental; she was always talking about what was wrong with the world. She never helped with the dishes or anything else. She was always going into the refrigerator and eating the last piece of pie or cheesecake or whatever dessert was there. She'd say weird things, and when you'd ask her to explain what she meant, she'd say, 'Oh, never mind.' She'd sit around looking as if somebody had been beating her with a stick. She'd droop on the wall. She was depressing.

In September, Lily would sit with her books on the floor of the den at night, reading and underlining sentences with fat turquoise lines. Virginia would be on the couch reading the paper, her square brown glasses on the end of her nose. The TV would be on, usually a talk show neither of them wanted to see. On the coffee table there'd be a fat economy-size jar of olives, which they both ate from. They'd talk intermittently, and Virginia liked to think that her silent presence was an encouragement to Lily's studying.

In September, Lily got good grades on her quizzes. Her art teacher said nice things about her drawings. She got an A-plus on a humanities paper, and the teacher read it aloud to the class. Virginia called Anne and read it to her.

During October, Lily stopped studying on the floor of the den. She left her broken-backed books on the couch and went upstairs to her room and shut the door. Virginia could hear the radio playing behind the door for hours. She wondered irritably what Lily was doing in there.

On weekends her long-haired friends would come to the door and she'd disappear for the entire day. At night they'd hear the screen door slam, and Lily would pat through the den, her bell-bottoms swishing, her face distantly warm and airy. She'd float down the hall without a word.

The second week in October, Mr Shin, the school disciplinarian, called Virginia. He told her that Lily was rude in the classroom and that she used obscene language. Two weeks later he called again, this time to say that he thought Lily was taking drugs.

Virginia thought Mr Shin had a repulsive voice. She thought he was deliberately persecuting Lily for reasons having nothing to do with obscene language or drugs. Lily once said that Mr Shin told her that her IQ was below normal, that she belonged in a mental hospital, and that he didn't blame her parents for not wanting her. At first Virginia was angry. She thought of telling Jarold to call Mr Shin and tell him to leave Lily alone. But then she realized that Jarold was in agreement with him. Then she felt embarrassed. After all, Mr Shin was right, Lily did use obscene language, casually and often. She did take drugs.

It was Lily's birthday. Jarold was out of town on business. Daniel and Charles had bought her a deck of tarot cards and a pair of earrings. There was a boxed cake in the refrigerator. Virginia was going to ask Lily what she wanted for dinner, but when Lily came home she was too high to answer the question. She tried to act normal, but she couldn't. She said weird things and giggled. Lily almost never giggled; it was a strangely unpleasant sound.

Virginia sent the boys to visit their friends next door. Then she turned to Lily. 'You are a constant irritant,' she said. 'I'll never forgive Anne for dumping you on me, although the poor woman was probably desperate to get rid of you.' She didn't remember what she said after that. She was furious, so it probably wasn't very nice. She recalled that Lily said nothing, that she seemed to shrink and become concave. She kept pulling her hair in front of her mouth and holding it there.

It was very different from the way Magdalen had acted when Virginia would catch her on drugs. Virginia could scream at Magdalen, and call her anything she liked. Magdalen would follow her around, her long legs working in big strides, eyes blazing. She'd yell, 'Mom! Mom, you know that's a bunch of shit. What about the time you . . .'

But Lily just sat there, becoming more and more expressionless.

Virginia slept with Lily that night. She went into her room, no longer angry but with a sense of duty, concerned that Lily know she was cared for, that she wouldn't go through the drug experience alone.

She found her lying on the bed with all her clothes on, staring. Virginia made her change into her nightgown and get under the blankets. She turned out the light and got into bed with her. Lily went into a tight curl and turned her face to the wall. Virginia got the impression that she didn't understand why Virginia was there.

Virginia said, 'Well? Don't you want to talk?'

Lily didn't answer for a long time. Then she said, 'About what?'

'Whatever's on your mind.'

Another long pause.

'There's nothing on my mind.'

Her words sounded disconnected, not only from her but from each other. Virginia suddenly wanted her to go home, back to Michigan. It would be easy. All she had to do was tell Jarold that she'd been taking drugs.

'Well, that's funny. Magdalen was a talker.'

'About what? What did she talk about?' She sounded genuinely interested.

'Oh, about boys. There was one in particular. David. I remember the name because she kept moaning it over and over.' She hadn't meant to sound sarcastic, but it was hard not to.

Lily didn't say anything.

They lay there in silence, not even scratching or shifting. Every time one of them swallowed, it was obvious that she was trying to do it quietly. Virginia's nightgown was hot and her feet were dry. She felt as if she couldn't close her eyes. She remembered the afternoon conversations they had shared and their walks in the mountains. They seemed meaningless now – like bits of color glimpsed through a kaleidoscope. She felt an unhappy chill.

Virginia turned, and the blankets rasped in the long silence. In a fiercely sudden move, she put her body against Lily's, and her arm around her. She waited, almost frightened.

For several seconds there was no reaction. Then Virginia could feel every muscle in Lily's body slowly tightening. Lily's body became rigid. Her back began to sweat.

They lay like that, uncomfortably, for a long time. Having moved, it was hard for Virginia to turn away again.

The next day they ate birthday cake from paper plates on their laps as they watched TV. Jarold said, 'Well, do you feel fifteen?'

'I don't know,' said Lily.

It seemed like she really didn't know. She looked badly shaken. Jarold didn't say anything else. Charles stopped eating his cake and looked at Lily for a long moment. He looked puzzled and disturbed; for one thing, Lily loved cake and she hadn't eaten any of the cake in her lap.

*

Virginia didn't tell Jarold about the drugs, but he got rid of Lily anyway. She had stayed out with her friends one night, and he had her things packed when she came back the next morning. They drove her to the airport within the hour and left her waiting for a standby flight with her clothes in a big white shopping bag. Virginia kissed her good-bye, but it didn't feel like anything.

That night Anne called. Lily had not gone home. She had taken a plane to Canada instead. 'I don't think we'll send anybody after her this time,' said Anne. 'It wouldn't do any good. Nothing we ever did was any good.'

'Don't blame yourself,' said Virginia.

For a few days afterward, Jarold talked about how awful it had been to have Lily there. Then he forgot about it. Charles was the last person to mention her. It was shortly after Virginia got a call from Magdalen. He said, 'You and Dad were always acting like Lily and Magdalen were alike. But they weren't anything alike at all.'

For a while after that, life was okay. Magdalen was still acting like an idiot, but seemed to have stabilized in a harmless way; she had a steady job as a waitress in a health-food restaurant in South Carolina, and talked about astral travel and crystal healing when they called her. Camille was in law school at Harvard. She was engaged to a handsome, smiling med student. She sent glorious twelve-page letters to her mother on multi-colored stationery covered with purple or turquoise ink. She described her teachers and her friends. She wrote about how much she loved Kevin, how much she wanted to have children and a career. She recorded her dreams and the art exhibits she'd seen. Virginia imagined Camille sitting at her desk in class. Her legs were folded restfully before her, her body slouched with arrogant feminine ease, but her neck was erect and her large eyes watchful. She imagined her sitting at an outdoor café, her bony knees childishly tilted together under the table, her long hands draped on top of her warm coffee cup as she leaned forward, laughing with her friends. She saw Camille walking across campus with Kevin. His brown jacket was loose on her shoulders, protecting her.

Daniel and Charles grew up easily. They trooped around the house with noisy bunches of boys who all seemed to have light, swinging arms and stinging, nasty voices. At times their eyes were dull and brutish. They told cruel, violent jokes and killed animals. They were mean to other children. But they harbored a sweetness and vulnerability that became exposed at unexpected moments. And they were still her little boys. She could hear it in the way Charles called, 'Mom?' when he couldn't sleep at night. She would pass by his room and hear his voice float plaintively from the darkness. She would look in and see him sitting up in his gray-and-white pajamas, slim and spare against the headboard, his blond hair standing up in pretty spikes. She would sit on his bed for at least an hour. Sometimes she would lift up his pajama top and gently scratch his warm back. He loved that.

When Daniel was fifteen, he found a girlfriend. She was fourteen. She was very short and had dark hair and gentle hands. She had a round, sweet face and worried eyes. She worried about things like ecology. She sat in the kitchen with Daniel after school, eating Virginia's sandwiches and talking about the EPA and whales. Her feet, in striped tennis shoes, barely touched the floor. Daniel admired her as he ate his sandwich. He stopped killing squirrels with BB guns.

When Charles was twelve, he was in a school play. He was one of the Lost Boys in the high school production of *Peter Pan*, a boy named Tootles. It was a small part, and he was nonchalant about it, but he loved to dress in his contrived rags and make his eyes fiendish with black eye paint. He came home from rehearsal that way. Virginia would see a beam of light in the driveway, then hear a car door slam and muffled voices. The door would bang and Charles would appear, nimbly swaggering in his frayed knickers and flapping sleeves. He'd grab something to eat from the kitchen and wheel into the den, yelling his lines in a mocking voice. 'You see, sir, I don't think my mother would like me to be a pirate. Would your mother like you to be a pirate, Slightly?'

She went to the play on opening night and sat in the front row with Jarold and Daniel. Charles was vibrant on stage. His airy movements had more authority than anyone else's in the cast, except the lead. She couldn't take her eyes off him. The pale little girl playing Wendy lay fainting before him in her white nightgown, her long brown hair fanned across his feet. He said, 'When ladies used to come to me in dreams I said, "Pretty mother, pretty mother." But when at last she really came, I shot her.' Tears came to her eyes. She looked at Jarold and saw him smiling and blinking rapidly. Charles said, 'I know I am just Tootles and nobody minds me. But the first who does not behave to Wendy like an English gentleman, I will blood him severely.'

When the play ended, Virginia went to the dressing room. It was an old classroom with heavy wooden mirrors propped against the walls and cardboard boxes full of makeup and cold cream on the desks. Children were leaping around the room, chattering and singing songs from the play in sarcastic voices. They were bright-eyed and demonic when seen up close. Virginia saw Charles. She saw him dip his hand into a jar of cold cream, turn and slap it across a timid-looking girl's face. The girl smiled painfully and tried to laugh. Another girl pointed at her and laughed. Charles turned away.

She dreamed of a conversation with Lily. They were sitting at the kitchen table with cups of tea before them. She said, 'After I had Daniel, the doctors told me that I shouldn't have any more children. They said it would be unsafe. I was lying there in the hospital when they came in and announced, "While we've got you here, we're going to tie your tubes." And I said, "Oh, no, you're not." I wouldn't let them do it. And the next year I had Charles.' She smiled foolishly at Lily.

The dream-Lily smiled back. 'Charles is a beautiful boy,' she said. 'I think he may be a genius in a way people don't yet understand.'

'Don't ever tell Daniel or Jarold I said this, but Charles is my favorite child. He's precious and special. Whenever I think of someone trying to harm him – any of my children really, but especially him – I picture myself turning into a mother tiger and lashing out. I would do anything to protect him.'

'Why would you think of anyone trying to harm him?' asked Lily. 'Just out of the blue?'

She woke up feeling guilty and frightened and

angry at Lily. She dimly tried to sort it out. Why should she feel any of these things? The doctors hadn't tried to tie her tubes. There had been no conversation with Lily. She went back to sleep.

When Daniel was sixteen, he had another girl-friend. She was another small girl, with dark hair and light-brown glasses. She wrote poetry and talked a lot about feminism. Virginia still had a snapshot of them on their way to the junior prom. The girl looked embarrassed and distressed in her gown and corsage. Daniel was indifferently handsome.

Charles became a delicate, pretty adolescent. His eyes were large and green and long-lashed, his neck slender. He slouched like an arrogant little cat. Girls got crushes on him, they called and asked to speak to him in scared, high-pitched voices. He was rude to them and hung up. The only girl he liked was a homely, jittery kid who wore a leather jacket and bleached her hair. But that ended when the girl was sent to some kind of institution.

Camille got married a month after she graduated. She and Kevin flew to New Jersey for the wedding. They posed for snapshots in the den. They were radiant against the jumbled background of random shoes and scattered newspapers.

Everybody walked around the house talking and laughing and eating hunks of white cake. Kevin's father shook hands with Jarold. Kevin's mother helped in the kitchen.

Camille and Kevin went to Spain for their honeymoon. Then they moved to New York and got jobs. Camille wrote letters on heavy gray stationery with 'Dr and Mrs Kevin Spaulding' printed across the top.

Magdalen was married the following spring. She married a Southern lawyer whom she had waited on in the health-food restaurant.

'Wouldn't you know it?' said Anne. 'She probably did it to shock you. She couldn't have Camille getting all the attention.'

'It's what she wanted all along,' said Betty. 'A daddy.'

John was ten years older than Magdalen. He was broad-shouldered and slow-moving, with lazy gray eyes. Magdalen cuddled against him, her hand quiet on his lapel.

Jarold watched them with deep approval. It relaxed him to talk about them or look at them.

Virginia was happy that Magdalen had found someone normal to take care of her. She was proud of her daughter's wedding beauty and of her successful husband. She enjoyed a smug feeling of vindication now that Magdalen had come to such a conventional end.

The couple moved to John's farm in North Carolina. Magdalen baked bread and kept house. She had a baby, a fat boy named Griffin. Virginia took snapshots of Magdalen holding Griffin in a ball of blankets, her eyes startled and glistening wildly above her grin. John stood over her, his chin held high, smiling his slow-eyed smile. Magdalen asked her for advice in a meek, thrilled voice.

Virginia called Anne. 'I love it,' she said. 'He doesn't let her get away with anything. If she gets high-toned, he puts her right in her place. And she *loves* it.'

Daniel graduated from high school and then went to college to study engineering. He went with heavy sweaters, socks and boxes of records. Virginia took a picture of him standing at the train station in a huge cream-colored sweater. His tennis-shoed feet were tight together, his shoulders were hunched. He smiled tolerantly into space as a long strand of blond hair blew across his forehead and licked the lashes of one eye.

Virginia stood in the kitchen and did the dishes in the afternoon. She wore a sweatshirt and loose slacks and fat gray socks. Her hair was in a high, wispy ponytail. The sun was warm and her hands were warm in the lightly food-flecked water. The radio was on, playing love songs, songs about babies and homes. Virginia sang as she washed, about roses and bluebirds and tears of joy. She knew they were stupid songs, but they made her feel exalted. They were notations for things too important and mysterious to describe accurately in radio songs.

They had barbecues in the evenings. They ate steak and potatoes and oily salad with flowery leaves. They ate regally in their lawn chairs, looking out into their big back yard and all the trees. Charles and Jarold argued about what Charles should do after high school, or whether New York was ugly or not. Charles usually said, 'Oh, never mind,' and kept eating. When he was finished, he got up to walk to the stream that ran in the wooded area behind their house. Virginia and Jarold sat alone, full and splendid, their jackets around their shoulders.

Virginia loaded the dishwasher in the dimly lit kitchen, scraping the bones and greasy napkins into big black garbage bags. There was TV noise from the den, and the low rasping sound that Jarold made when he moved the newspaper. Charles came in, his face distant, his light jacket flapping. She circled his head with her arm, brought it to her shoulder and held it there to kiss before he broke from her and went away down the hall.

She sometimes sat on the couch with a pile of vinyl photo albums. One album opened on her lap to show a glanceful of red snowsuits, Christmas trees, armloads of grinning dolls, and beautiful tall children who smiled, drew pictures and were happy. Holding Easter baskets full of grass and chocolate. Raking the leaves. Winning trophies. The weddings and the graduations. The long-ribboned corsages.

She had to remind herself that Anne and Betty had families that were nice in other ways, that one of Betty's daughters was a certified genius and went to a school for advanced children.

She wrote to Anne and told her, 'We're getting fat and sassy.'

It was winter when Camille called. She asked how Virginia was doing and waited while Virginia told her. She asked about Magdalen and the boys. Then she said, 'Mother, I'm having an abortion.'

Virginia stifled a choking noise. 'Were you raped?' she managed to ask.

Camille began to cry. 'No,' she said.

Virginia waited as Camille controlled her voice.

'No,' said Camille. 'Kevin doesn't want to have children. I let myself get pregnant without telling him. I thought he would change his mind, but he didn't. He's really mad. He says if I don't have an abortion, he'll divorce me.'

Virginia left the phone feeling very unlike herself.

She made a cup of tea and went into the den with it. She sat on the couch with one gray-socked foot propped up on the coffee table. She wondered why Kevin didn't want to have children.

She did not tell Jarold about the abortion.

Camille came home to visit. She walked around the house in her old snakeskin jumpsuit, her little hips twitching briskly. She told stories about being a corporate lawyer and teased 'Daddy.' Virginia admired her. But she noticed the stiff grinning lines around her mouth.

Camille visited Magdalen too. She stayed with her for two days before flying back to New York. She wrote Virginia a letter shortly afterward and told her that she felt something strange was happening between John and Magdalen. Magdalen was brittle, she said. John ordered her around a lot, in a very nasty way. She said that late one night she woke up and heard the sound of someone being rhythmically and repeatedly slapped. It went on for about five minutes. Magdalen looked fine the next day, and Camille had been too embarrassed to say anything.

Virginia called Magdalen late that night, when Jarold was in bed. She didn't hear anything strange in her voice. When Virginia got off the phone, she put on an old gray sweater and walked from room to room. The rooms were dark and hollow. They seemed unfamiliar and eerie, but that didn't make her go upstairs or turn on the light. She stood in the middle of the dark living room with her feet together, wrapping the sweater around her. She stood there not thinking about anything, just hearing the wind and the faint hum of the house.

Charles and Jarold had a fight. Charles was graduating from high school and he didn't want to go to college. He just wanted to move out of the house. Jarold told him his attitude was stupid and weak. 'Magdalen thought she'd go the unconventional, freaky route,' said Jarold at breakfast, 'and look where it got her. Married, a mother. And happy for the first time in her mixed-up life.'

'I still think Magdalen's freaky,' said Charles.

It went on for about a week. Then Charles lost his temper. He said, 'I'd rather be on my face in the Bowery than be a horse's ass like you.'

'Charles,' said Virginia.

Jarold crossed the room and belted Charles across the face, knocking him out of his chair. Virginia dropped her glass in the sink and ran to Charles. 'Don't you dare hit my son!' she screamed.

'Oh, get out of here, you idiot,' said Charles. He wiped the blood from his mouth in a bored way.

*

Virginia began sitting up late at night in the den, drinking and staring at her gray feet. She made sarcastic comments that nobody paid any attention to. Jarold called her 'Mother.' 'Now, Mother,' he'd say.

Charles moved to New York. He got a job in a record store and an apartment on the Lower East Side of Manhattan. Other than that, it was hard to tell what he was doing.

Virginia called Camille. Camille was meeting wonderful new people and being successful. She told lots of funny stories. But then she said, 'I don't know if I should tell you this, but I'm having a hard time keeping it to myself. Last month Magdalen told me that John slapped her. Not hard or anything. But still.'

She paused so Virginia could say something. Virginia sat quietly and stared at the kitchen.

'Of course, we both know how annoying Magdalen can be,' continued Camille. 'But that doesn't give him the right to strike her.'

Virginia left the conversation feeling cheated. Camille had told her about Magdalen at the end of the conversation, after all the good things. That seemed strange to Virginia. She sat for a long time on the stool under the phone with her legs tightly crossed and her elbows on the knee of one leg. She thought about how awful the kitchen was. There were balls of dust and tiny crumbs around the edges of the floor. Pans full of greasy water ranged across the counter. The top of the refrigerator was black. Everything in the room seemed disconnected from its purpose.

In the fall, Daniel decided that he didn't like engineering school and dropped out. Jarold argued with him over the phone for a long time. When he hung up, Jarold went out into the garage and sat in the car with a scarf around his neck. He sat there for over an hour. Virginia could hear the car's engine start, chug awkwardly, and then shut off. This happened several times. She couldn't tell whether Jarold was repeatedly deciding to drive somewhere and then changing his mind, or if he was just keeping warm.

Camille divorced Kevin two months later. She put her things in bags and boxes and moved into a girlfriend's apartment. She tried to make it sound like fun. Virginia pictured her sitting on the couch with her friend, both of them bundled in blankets, drinking mugs of tea, being supportive. It was a nice picture, but it seemed adolescent.

Everybody came home for the holidays. Magdalen and Camille hugged each other constantly during the visit. On Christmas they wore their pajamas and slippers all day. They sat close together and squeezed each other's hands. They had confidential conversations, which Virginia only half heard. When they talked to anyone else, their faces stiffened slightly. Magdalen had a hard time finishing a sentence.

No one else seemed to notice. 'Magdalen's always been flighty,' said Jarold.

Charles was very pale. He picked at the Christmas meal, eating very little. His dinner plate was a mass of picked-apart food. Daniel ate a lot. He ate while he talked or walked through the room. There were often light brown crumbs on his plaid shirt.

Virginia took only one group picture. It came out ugly. Magdalen's eyes were a dazed green slur. Camille's neck was rigid and stretched, her eyes bulged. Daniel's eyes were rolled up and his nostrils were flared. Charles hung back on the couch, his hand covering the face of a malignant elf. Jarold, half in the picture and seen from the side, was frozen in the middle of a senseless gesture.

Virginia and Jarold were in the den watching the late movie when Magdalen called. Virginia tried to ignore the phone. It rang eight times. 'Are you going to get that, honey?' said Jarold.

Magdalen's voice was calm. 'Mama, I'm calling from the bus station in Charleston. John and I had a fight. He broke my nose. Griffin and I are coming home.'

She arrived at 4:30 in the morning. Virginia stood at the door in a flannel nightgown watching the taxi pull into the driveway. Magdalen emerged in the open-car-door light, a thin girl in a bulky army coat. The door shut and she became a slow, bundled figure kicking the driveway gravel with her shuffling steps. 'Mom?' Her voice was sheepish and sweet.

She carried one suitcase and a big shopping bag. Griffin had just started walking. He looked tired and wistful. His blond hair was much too long.

John called the house, but they hung up on him. He threatened to come and get Magdalen, but Jarold said he'd kill him if he did.

Magdalen found a small apartment in town. She got a job at a flower shop. Virginia took care of Griffin during the day while Magdalen was at work. Griffin was a shy, pensive child who talked in bursts. He was precise, analytical and watchful. He made Virginia feel protective and sad. She tried hard to keep her sadness from showing.

After a few months the florist let Magdalen take the flowers home so she could be with Griffin.

On weekends Magdalen and Virginia went shopping for clothes or groceries. They were quiet and easy with each other. Magdalen lent Virginia books to read, and they talked about them.

Virginia was surprised at how nice it was to be in Magdalen's apartment. She liked to go there in the mornings with cherry-cheese pastry or fruit. Magdalen would be in the large, bare main room, sitting in her cotton robe on a floor pillow. The sun would come in through a big, curtainless window. There were white plastic buckets of roses, tulips, irises, freesia, dyed carnations, birds of paradise and wild magenta daisies. There were bunches of flowers on the floor on wet, unrolled newspaper. Stripped rose thorns lay on the paper like lost baby teeth.

Magdalen's movements were nimble and quick. Her face was serene and beautiful. She seemed completely content.

Virginia felt as though she were a total stranger.

Virginia and Jarold became very quiet together. They still watched late-night movies, but they rarely sat cuddled together. Jarold got tired early and went upstairs to bed. He was always asleep when Virginia came up.

Sometimes she thought Jarold looked obtuse and stupid. At breakfast, when he bent over the paper, he frowned so hard that his mouth pulled his entire face downward and he looked like a shark. His eyes were disapproving. His nose became blunt as a snout.

She knew that he thought his children were failures.

*

Camille found a wonderful apartment. She began dating a man whom she liked a lot. She came to New Jersey often. She usually stayed with Magdalen. Virginia would take them all for a drive in the mountains. They ate ice cream and made family jokes. The girls would lie all over the back seat and giggle, Camille's hand on Magdalen's thigh, one tilting her head against the other's shoulder.

It was early morning when they found out about Charles. Jarold had just gotten into the shower. The clock radio, wavering between two stations, interlaced the weather report with a song about dumping your girlfriend. Virginia felt her forehead wrinkling as she tried to ignore the noise. She burrowed her head into the pillow and listened to the warm, dull whish of the shower. The phone rang. She opened her eyes; the red digits said 6:15. She wouldn't have answered if it hadn't kept ringing so long.

He had been driving from upstate New York in a friend's car. He had been drinking. He'd passed a truck coming around a turn, collided with another car and gone off the road. His car flipped over and caught fire. His car was badly burned. The other driver survived.

*

Virginia's life became a set of events with no meaning or relationship to one another. She was a cold planet orbiting for no reason in a galaxy of remote, silent movement. The house was a series of objects that she had to avoid bumping into. Food would not go down her throat. The faces of her husband and children were abstract patterns taking on various shapes to symbolize various messages. It was exhausting to keep track of them.

She slept on the couch in the den every night. At first it just happened that way. She'd be sitting before the TV with her glass of Scotch when Jarold would kiss the top of her head and go upstairs. She'd go into the kitchen and get a bottle and drink from it. She'd watch the chartreuse-and-violet people walk around the screen. It was sometimes a comfort.

She fell asleep on the hard little throw pillow. She always woke up with sweat around her collar and a stiff neck.

One night Jarold took her hand and said, 'Come on, honey. Come to bed. You'll fall asleep on the couch if you don't.'

'I want to fall asleep on the couch,' said Virginia.

'No, you don't,' said Jarold. He tugged her arm. 'It's unhealthy. Come into your nice warm bed.'

She yanked her hand out of his. 'I don't want to sleep in the bed.'

It was true. She couldn't bear the thought of lying next to him. He could see it in her eyes and it wounded him. He walked away. He said nothing about it again.

Magdalen came to see her almost every day. She walked around the kitchen cleaning things while Virginia sat at the table. Virginia watched her long, calm hands closing cabinets, sorting silverware, rubbing surfaces with wet, stained old cloths. She remembered how Magdalen used to run around and make so much noise. It was a clear memory, but it didn't seem as though it was hers.

Virginia began getting up to cook Jarold's breakfast again. She put an extra alarm clock beside the couch. She put on a robe over her rumpled clothes and moved around the kitchen. She put her plate of eggs opposite Jarold's and ate them. Jarold's jaws chewed stiffly; his throat was like wood. But they talked, and she found it comforting.

Before he left he would hold her hand and kiss her. She'd wait until he was gone, then sit back down again and cry.

Charles had been dead eight months when Anne came.

Virginia drove to the airport to pick her up. It was strange to be at the wheel of a car again, driving with a lot of other cars around her. It was very sunny, and the primary-colored metal of the cars was festive in the brightness. She turned the radio on and rolled down the window.

Anne was waiting at the terminal in a gray suit. When she saw Virginia she tipped her head to the side and grinned; she raised her hand and waved it in stiff, frantic waves.

They hugged. Anne only came up to Virginia's chest. Still hugging, they leaned back to look at each other and laughed. Anne's glasses were cockeyed. 'Goodness, you've gotten thin,' she said. 'Let's take you home and feed you. I'm starved.'

They rode through traffic, chattering. Virginia didn't go straight home. She left the highway and drove up into the mountains. Anne rolled down her window and put her gray elbow on the ledge. She said, 'It's simply glorious up here.'

They had egg sandwiches and fruit for lunch. Virginia had cleaned the kitchen and put a vase of pink and white carnations on the table. The fruit was cut up in a large cream-colored bowl. They helped themselves at a leisurely pace, sometimes eating the wet, lightly bruised fruit straight from the bowl with their fingers. The afternoon sun came in, lighting up a sparkling flurry of dust flecks.

*

Virginia talked about Camille, Daniel and Magdalen. She told Anne about Camille's career success and about how helpful Magdalen was. 'She still lives like a hippie, though. I don't think she misses the big ranch they had at all. She certainly doesn't miss John. The only time she's ever mentioned him was to say that she was always surprised at how stupid he turned out to be. It's weird. It's like it never happened.'

'Well, you know some people work best in that kind of footloose life-style,' said Anne. 'It's called being a bohemian. Lily's still that way.'

'Is she doing well?'

'Oh, yes. You know, I don't ever worry about her anymore. Ever since she's gotten serious about photography, her whole life's pulled together. She really works hard. She works for all the papers and magazines in Detroit.'

Virginia looked at the pieces of fruit on her plate. 'I always thought that Lily could do well if she wanted to,' she said. 'She was such a sensitive child. I was sorry I couldn't do anything to help her.'

'Don't feel that way. You couldn't have done anything. She was too difficult.'

'Yes,' said Virginia. 'She was.'

'But she has good memories of you,' said Anne. 'She used to tell me about going up into the mountains with you. She said that the two of you ate so many olives in the living room together that for years the color of olives made her think of you.' Anne grinned in a hideously open way.

Virginia looked at the fruit.

'And then do you know what she said? She said, "But that's not right because Virginia's not like an olive color at all. She's more golden."'

'Oh, stop it,' said Virginia.

'But that's how I always thought of you too, even when you were awful. You were always golden.'

Anne was smiling again, her eyes in sad half-moons. She saw that Virginia was embarrassed, so she looked down and picked up a wet piece of melon. She ate it, smiling dimly. The movements of her jaw were neat and careful.

Virginia was afraid for a moment that she was going to say something nasty to Anne, though she wasn't sure why. She had a drink of coffee instead. It was getting cold and oily.

'What's wrong?' Anne was watching her with a dark, naked look.

Virginia glanced away. 'Nothing.'

They had an old-fashioned family barbecue for Anne's visit. It was the first one they'd had in a year, and Jarold was excited about it. He was ceremonious and manly beside the smoking barbecue, pronged fork in hand.

Anne nervously mixed the salad and talked to Jarold about her job counseling old people in Detroit. Magdalen came out of the house, bringing a flat dish of cold pasta. She put the dish on the card table and her hand on Virginia's shoulder. 'How are you doing, Mama? Did you and Anne have a good time?'

'We had a lovely time. We went for a long drive in the mountains.'

'Oh, yes,' said Anne. 'We actually got out of the car and *walked* for a long time. I was enthralled. It was just gorgeous.'

'Anne must've put a pound of rocks in her pockets,' said Virginia. 'Every time I turned around, she was picking up something else.'

'I love it up there,' said Magdalen. 'It's my salvation.' She moved lightly around the card table, folding napkins.

'You know, something I've noticed since I've gotten older is my sensitivity to nature,' said Anne. 'When I was very young – a teenager – the sight of a sunset or a mountain scene was so deeply moving to me, I would get the chills.' She looked at Magdalen and shivered her shoulders. 'And then, as I entered my twenties, I lost that sensitivity.'

'Well, I'm sure it wasn't lost. You just had to concentrate on other things,' said Virginia.

'I suppose,' said Anne. 'But there came a point when

I hardly responded to nature at all. I still liked it, but it didn't move me. Now that I'm on the verge of becoming an old lady, I'm starting to respond to nature again, to be stirred by the great outdoors.' She looked at Jarold with vulnerable eyes, her glasses down on her nose.

'That's wonderful,' he said. 'It shows you're still excited by life. And that's the most important thing to keep through the years, more important than money or success. A lot of us lose it.'

'I believe that,' said Anne. 'That's why I enjoy working with old folks. It's marvelous to watch some of them blossom again, especially the ones who've been in those horrible nursing homes. They can be like kids with the openness – it's exciting to give them another chance to experience it.'

'You're a very giving person,' said Jarold. He looked at Anne with tender, protective awe, a little shamed, as if he knew that giving was beyond his ability but he was glad that somebody was there to do it.

It was strange to Virginia. When they were young, Jarold thought Anne was silly and too serious and a frump besides. Now here he was, thirty years later, looking at her like that.

'The steaks are ready,' said Jarold.

Magdalen put the steaks on the plates. Anne and Virginia arranged servings of salad and pasta. They all sat in lawn chairs and ate from the warm plates in their laps. The steak was good and rare; its juices ran into the salad and pasta when Virginia moved her knees. A light wind blew loose hairs around their faces and tickled them. The trees rustled dimly. There were nice insect noises.

Jarold paused, a forkful of steak rising across his chest. 'Like heaven,' he said. 'It's like heaven.'

They were quiet for several minutes.

About the Authors

Candice Brathwaite is an acclaimed author, journalist, and TV presenter, with over 244k Instagram followers. Her first book, *I Am Not Your Baby Mother*, made it to the *Sunday Times* best-seller list, and her first foray into fiction, the YA novel *Cuts Both Ways*, was published in August 2022. Candice is a Contributing Editor at *Grazia* and frequently appears on national radio and television, including regular appearances on *Steph's Packed Lunch*.

Lydia Davis is the author of one novel and six short-story collections, the most recent of which was a finalist for the 2007 National Book Award. She is the recipient of a MacArthur Fellowship and was named a Chevalier of the Order of Arts and Letters by the French government for her fiction and her translations of modern writers, including Gustave Flaubert and Marcel Proust. She won the Man Booker International Prize in 2013.

Anita Desai was born and educated in India, is the author of many novels and short stories and has been shortlisted for the Booker Prize three times for her novels *Clear Light of Day*, *In Custody* and *Fasting, Feasting*. She is the Emerita John E. Burchard Professor of Humanities at the Massachusetts Institute of Technology and a Fellow of both the American Academy of Arts and the Royal Society of Literature.

Mary Gaitskill is the author of the story collections *Bad Behavior*, *Because They Wanted To* (nominated for the PEN/Faulkner Award), and *Don't Cry*, the novels *The Mare*, *Veronica* (nominated for the National Book Award), *Two Girls, Fat and*

Thin and a collection of essays, *Somebody with a Little Hammer*. Her stories and essays have appeared in the *New Yorker*, *Harper's Bazaar*, and *Granta*, among many other journals, as well as in *The Best American Short Stories*.

Jamaica Kincaid was born in St John's, Antigua. Her books include *A Small Place*, *At the Bottom of the River*, *Annie John*, *Lucy*, *The Autobiography of My Mother* and *My Brother*. She lives with her family in Vermont.

Toni Morrison was awarded the Nobel Prize in Literature in 1993. She was the author of many novels, including *The Bluest Eye*, *Sula*, *Beloved*, *Paradise* and *Love*. She received the National Book Critics Circle Award and a Pulitzer Prize for her fiction and was awarded the Presidential Medal of Freedom, America's highest civilian honour, in 2012 by Barack Obama. Toni Morrison died on 5 August 2019 at the age of eighty-eight.

Ngũgĩ wa Thiong'o is one of the leading writers and scholars at work in the world today. He has authored more than thirty books, including novels, short stories, memoirs, essays and children's books. His novel *Petals of Blood* saw him imprisoned by the Kenyan government in 1977. Recipient of many honours, among them ten honorary doctorates, Ngũgĩ wa Thiong'o is currently distinguished professor of English and Comparative Literature at the University of California, Irvine.

Irenosen Okojie is an experimental Nigerian British author. Her books have won and been nominated for multiple awards. Her journalism has been featured in the *New York Times*, *Observer*, *Guardian* and *Huffington Post*. She co-presents the BBC's *Turn Up For The Books* podcast alongside Simon Savidge and Bastille frontman, Dan Smith. Vice chair of the Royal Society of Literature, she was awarded an MBE for services to literature in 2021.

Tabitha Siklos is a writer and researcher from Surrey. She has a Masters in Creative Writing from Birkbeck College, University of

London. She worked for a decade as a lawyer and, following stints as a blogger and ghostwriter, she is currently a researcher on the authorised biography of Stephen Hawking. Having a trio of small children, Tabitha's fiction and non-fiction examines (among other themes), the wondrous gore and glory of motherhood. 'Foetus' was shortlisted for the *White Review* Short Story Prize.

Helen Simpson's sixth short-story collection, *Cockfosters*, follows *Four Bare Legs in a Bed, Dear George, Hey Yeah Right Get a Life, Constitutional* and *In-Flight Entertainment*. *A Bunch of Fives: Selected Stories* includes five stories from each of her first five collections. She has received the *Sunday Times* Young Writer of the Year Award, the Somerset Maugham Award, the Hawthornden Prize and the E. M. Forster Award. She lives in London.

Ali Smith was born in Inverness in 1962. She has written sixteen novels and been shortlisted for the Booker Prize, Orange Prize and Orwell Prize. Her novel *How to be Both* won the Bailey's Prize, the Goldsmiths Prize and the Costa Novel of the Year Award, and was shortlisted for the Man Booker Prize. Ali Smith lives in Cambridge.

Tessa Hadley is the author of eight highly praised novels, the most recent of which is *Free Love*. *The Past* won the Hawthornden Prize in 2016, while *Bad Dreams* won the 2018 Edge Hill Short Story Prize. She also won a Windham-Campbell prize for Fiction in 2016. Her short stories appear regularly in the *New Yorker*.

Casey Plett is the author of *A Dream of a Woman, Little Fish* and *A Safe Girl to Love*. She has written for the *New York Times, Guardian, Harper's Bazaar* and other publications. A winner of the Amazon First Novel Award, the Firecracker Award for Fiction, and a two-time winner of the Lambda Literary Award, her work has also been nominated for the Scotiabank Giller Prize. She currently splits her time between New York City and Windsor, Ontario.

Acknowledgements

Vintage Classics gratefully acknowledges permission to reprint copyright material as follows:

'What You Learn About the Baby' from *Varieties of Disturbance* by Lydia Davis (Hamish Hamilton, 2010), copyright © Lydia Davis 2009. Reprinted by permission of Penguin Random House Ltd.

'Winterscape' from *The Complete Stories* by Anita Desai (Chatto & Windus, 2017), copyright © Anita Desai 2017. Reprinted by permission of Rogers, Coleridge and White.

'Heaven' from *Bad Behavior* by Mary Gaitskill (Penguin Classics, 2008), copyright © Mary Gaitskill 1988. Reprinted by permission of Penguin Random House Ltd.

'Girl' from *At the Bottom of the River* by Jamaica Kincaid (Farrar, Straus and Giroux, 1983), copyright © Jamaica Kincaid 1978. Reprinted by permission of The Wylie Agency.

'Sweetness' by Toni Morrison (*New Yorker*, Vol. 90, no. 47. February 9, 2015. pp. 58–61), copyright © Toni Morrison 2015. Reprinted by permission of the Estate of Toni Morrison.

'Of Mothers and Children' from *Secret Lives and Other Stories* by Ngũgĩ wa Thiong'o (Vintage Classics, 2018), copyright © Ngũgĩ wa Thiong'o 1975. Reprinted by permission of Abner Stein.

penguin.co.uk/vintage-classics